Seven Kisses

A novel by DL Gallie

It was only meant to be a New Year's kiss for Huxley and Kendall, but one kiss wasn't enough.

Seven kisses was all it took for them to know they'd found their happily ever after.

It seemed simple enough, but fate kept pulling them apart.

They hoped to have forever, but they were about to find out, happily ever afters might only be for fairy tales.

Edited by **Karen Hrdlicka**, Barren Acres Editing

Cover Designed by **Tash Drake**, Outlined With Love Designs

Proofread by **Lisa Edwards**

Formatting and interior design by **DL Gallie**

DEDICATION

For Lana
Thank you for coming into my life.
Huxley is yours.

1

KENDALL

"ONCE UPON A TIME, a princess was awaiting her knight in shining armour to swoop in and..." Ugh, fairy tales are such bullshit, but for some reason little boys and girls love them. I'm reading this story of the princess and her knight with the fakest of fake enthusiasm. The cutie patootie currently lying next to me loves every word that's spewing out of my mouth, but most of all, he'd loved to be the knight in shining armour. Probably because after it being just him and his mom for so long, her knight, and his bio dad, finally got their HEA.

Sure, I have the dream job and an amazing seventh-floor apartment in downtown Vancouver, but my love life can be described in one word, shithouse. I never seem to find my white knight and no matter how many toads I kiss, they never turn into the handsome prince.

Looking down, I see that Harley is sound asleep. Sliding off the bed, I head out to the living room and take a seat on the sofa. Turning on Netflix, I start watching *The Notebook*. Another example of the path to unrequited love being bumpy. The last thing I remember is Rachel McAdams flapping her arms around on the beach being a bird. Now, the TV screen is black, a blanket has been draped over me and all the lights are out. Some babysitter I am, I didn't even hear them come home...and then I hear moans coming from the master bedroom, sure I hear THAT but not them arriving home. The moans grow louder and THAT'S my cue to leave.

Grabbing my things, quietly sneak out, order myself an Uber and head back to Luxe. I've been here in Hawaii for the last few weeks, assisting with the grand opening of the latest Luxe hotel. However, I really wasn't needed because Krista, mostly known as Sully, is a kick-ass marketing director and Hunter is an amazing CEO. Despite the hurdles thrown at them, they made this opening a total success, and I can see this hotel overtaking the one in Tahiti as the top Luxe hotel.

The next morning, I'm in my room packing when there's a knock at the door. Placing down my toiletry bag, I look through the peephole and smile when I see Sully standing there.

"Morning, Sully," I greet her as I swing the door open.

"You snuck out like a skanky ho," she says in place of a hello, shoving a venti caramel latte into my hand as she passes by and enters my suite—perks of working for the marketing department in a high-end resort.

"Well, with the boom-chicka-wow-wow noises coming from the master suite, I didn't feel comfortable staying."

Her eyes widen. "Oh.My.God, I'm so embarrassed. I told H you'd hear, but he does this thing with his tongue—"

"Lalalalalala," I singsong, "I don't need to hear anymore...I heard enough last night."

"Can we forget that ever happened and go get brunch before you leave? I'm gonna miss your face when you head back to Canada."

"I'm gonna miss you too. It feels like I've known you forever," I honestly tell her, and it's one-billion-percent true. She knows me as well as Rarns does, and Rarns and I have been friends since we were five.

"I know, right? And there's a little boy who is going to miss you too."

"And I'm gonna miss him. You've done a great job raising him, Sul, and now that you have H to help, he's going to grow up and be even more awesome."

"I hope so. I keep expecting to wake up and find out this is all a dream. I'm happier than I've ever been before, and I don't want to ever not feel like this."

"I'm sure there's an unwritten rule in fairy tales that once the HEA is officially locked in, it can never be broken."

"For someone who thinks fairy tales are bullshit, you certainly talk about them all the time."

Shrugging at her, I take a sip of my coffee and process

her words because she's right. A happily ever after isn't in the cards for me. Sure, I'm dating Chad right now, but is he my white knight? Or just another toad? Who knows, but what I do know, is that I love seeing others in love and getting their HEAs.

Hunter, Harley, and Sully drop me off at the airport. After I've checked in, I make my way through security and head toward my gate. Stopping at the bookstore, I grab a new read for the flight home, picking up *Montana Moonshine* by Vi Summers. I mean, who doesn't love a ruggedly hot cowboy and a felon? And hello, the cover is sexy as hell.

With my romance novel in hand, I wait at the departure gate to board my plane back to Vancouver. I glance around, taking it all in. People watching is so much fun at the best of times, but in an airport, it's epically fun. Right now, I'm creating a story in my head about the couple across from me. They look angry with one another and it's probably because they're currently leaving Hawaii, but I'm thinking it's because she hooked up with the maid and he's pissed he didn't get to watch the girl-on-girl action.

I'm really messed up in the head thinking that, but life's too boring to think normal things.

The hairs on the back of my neck prickle and a shiver runs up my spine. I've never felt like this before and then from the corner of my eye, I see movement. Turning my head, my eyes widen when I see *him*. I'm staring at the hottest guy I have ever seen, and I've been in Hawaii for the last three weeks...during summer. Where shirts are optional, and abs are a must. He races past the gate, and my head follows each stride he takes through the terminal. He turns his head, and our gaze briefly meets. Everything around me fades away. It's just him and me—great, now I'm gonna be singing that Halsey song all the way back to Canada—and within the blink of an eye, Hottie McHotterson is gone. Shaking my head, I look around and wonder if I just imagined him but before I can probe any further, my flight is called.

Like cattle we board the plane and I keep looking around for my hottie, but alas, he's not on this flight. See, fairy tales are bullshit. If this was a fairy tale, he would have been on my fight and sitting next to me. Or, I would have been upgraded to first-class and seated next to me was Prince Charming, and somewhere over the Pacific Ocean, we'd fall madly in love and live happily ever after. But noooo, I'm squished in between Smelly McSmellerson and Fatty McFatterson. Being sandwiched where I am proves that fairy tales and happily ever afters only exist in books and in the movies.

2

HUXLEY

...four months later
...New Year's Eve

THIS IS the first New Year's I don't have Hayden by my side as my wingman because he's now happily married to his soul mate. He hasn't ditched me completely, and I'm currently waiting for him and Bryce to join me here at Prohibition. I bet they're late because they're fucking like rabbits...like they always do.

Walking up to the bar, I smile when I see Embry working. "My man," I yell, garnering his attention.

"Westie," he greets me, offering his hand over the bar. "Haven't seen you around for a while."

"I've been doing back-to-backs, so I've been staying up in Alberta."

"I'll be sure to mark a reserved spot right here for you."

"Very funny but I totally appreciate the awesome service. I'll take a beer, thanks."

"Coming right up."

He slides my drink across to me. Lifting it to my lips, I chug back half the bottle, and Embry being the great A plus bartender that he is, has another one waiting for me.

"Thanks, man."

He nods and gets back to it. This place is usually packed and tonight, being New Year's Eve, is no exception. The tunes are pumping, and the atmosphere is already electric.

A tap on my shoulder garners my attention, and when I turn my head, I see my best friend's wife. "Bryce," I offer in greeting, kissing her on the cheek. "You look hawt."

This earns me a smack across the back of the head. "Stop flirting with my wife."

"Hayden," she berates him, "be nice."

"Yeah, Hayden, be nice," I taunt him, and I add to the taunting by pulling his wife into a hug, wrapping my arms around her waist, lifting her up, and spinning us around.

"Stop antagonizing him," she says with a slap to my head, just like her husband did a few moments ago. "And put me down, I need a mojito."

"Already on it, Cookie," Hayden says, handing me another beer.

"You trying to get me drunk?"

"Like you need my help."

"This is true, I've been getting myself drunk since I was sixteen."

"No wonder you're missing so many essential brain cells," Hayd teases.

"Says the one missing brain cells."

"My cells are just fine." He pulls his wife into his side. "My cells helped me win over this lucky lady right here." He kisses her on her temple, and there's nothing but love radiating between the two of them.

Pretending to gag, I roll my eyes. "Ugh, you two are so in love, it's disgusting."

"Mark my word, Huxley Weston," Bryce states matter-of-factly, "one of these days, you will meet someone, and she will knock you on your ass quicker than you've ever been knocked down before."

"You need to ease up on the mojitos, Bryce, you're drunk already."

"Not drunk, just stating a fact. When this one here," she flicks her thumb toward Hayden, "swooped into my life, it was a crazy whirlwind, but I knew, deep down, he was the one."

"But you two are meant to be."

"And you are meant to be with someone too. Your other half is out there, you just need to open your eyes." She looks to her husband. "Let's dance."

The two of them head out to the dance floor as Tones and I croon about dancing. Watching them dance, I process her words and wonder if she's right. Will I fall ass over tit when I least expect it?

Turning my gaze away from them, my eyes land on a woman. The woman of my dreams. Dark hair. Killer curves. Luscious lips. A smile that could light up a small town and gorgeous tits—not too big, not too small, just perfect. She's the complete package. I stand here and like a fucking creeper, I watch her.

My eyes are locked on the gorgeous brunette who's shaking her booty with her friend. Well, I hope it's her friend and not her lover. The two of them are seductively dancing together and every male in the room, straight or otherwise, is watching them. They continue to dance together and my mind drifts to the three of us together, and I begin to wonder if it *is* her lover and if maybe they'd be open to a little three-way fun this New Year's. I've never gone there before, but what guy doesn't want to have an amazing evening with two smoking hot chicks?

Leaning back against the bar, I sip on my beer and continue to watch them bump and grind up on each other. She spins around and lifts her head, our gaze connects, and everything around me fades away. It's just her, me, and Meghan Trainor singing about the bass. We have a whole conversation with just our eyes. My body comes alive at the intensity of her stare.

She breaks our stare off first and in the blink of an eye, she's gone. My eyes dart around, but it's as if she disappeared into thin air. Sighing dejectedly, I pick up my beer and take a swig. Sliding the empty across the bar, I pick up the one that Embry delivered while I was having my moment with dancing girl. Turning back around, I lean against the bar and look back to the dance floor, hoping to find dancing girl again.

Her friend is now grinding up on the guy behind her, so it looks like my three-way won't be happening after all, but it now gives me ample access to the hot brunette, if I can find her again.

3

KENDALL

ONCE AGAIN, it's New Year's Eve, and this year, I'm single...and not ready to mingle, but my best friend, Rani Murphy has dragged me out to celebrate the end of a shitty year and welcome in a new, hopefully, less shitty one.

Rani popped over earlier today with everything needed to transform me from heartbroken slob to sexy lady. We spent the afternoon in my apartment, drinking mimosas and pampering ourselves. I will admit, it was nice but I'm not telling her that.

For the last week, I've been moping about because my boyfriend, Chad, up and left me...for another man. How did I not know he was gay? When in reality it was waving its sparkly jazz hands in my face. It all started to turn to shit a few weeks ago when he proposed a threesome. I'm pretty open-minded, and what girl doesn't want to be pleasured by two hot naked guys? Exactly, but my ménage didn't quite happen like in my fantasies. You see, Chad and I ended up pleasuring *him*. After that night, our sex life started to dwindle, and then on Christmas Eve, Chad arrived at my place and told me that he was hopelessly in love with Tad, our threesome partner, and he was dumping me. And yes, they are now officially Chad and Tad.

Hence my wallowing for the past seven days.

When my brother, Kallen, found out, he wanted to fly back to Vancouver and beat him up. I told him not to because the season is in play, and I will not let Chad and Tad ruin his dream or cause my Crushers to lose because their star goalie was protecting his sister's honour. Kallen has worked too hard to get where he is, and I couldn't be prouder of my baby brother following his dreams; signing on as the goalie for the New York Crushers, making his childhood dream of playing in the NHL come true.

Besides, Chad really isn't worth it, and truth be told, I think I'm better off without him. Maybe...but I do miss his tongue. That man could really bring a girl immense pleasure with just his tongue...Tad is a lucky, lucky man.

So now, I'm standing at the bar, Prohibition, with my best friend, looking smoking hot...but wishing I was at home. I'm wearing black skinny jeans, a sparkly halter top that showcases the girls, and my signature sky-high, matte black stiletto heels. Heels are my jam, the higher the better but not so high that I don't look like a newborn calf when I walk. My makeup is simple, and my choco- late brown locks have been straightened flat and pulled up into a sexy high ponytail.

Rani grabs our complimentary wine from the server passing by and hands it to me. Placing it on the bar, I turn to face her and smile, she too looks hot tonight. She's

wearing a blood-red, skin-tight halter dress that accentuates her curves and makes her itty-bitty titties look bigger
than they are. She too is wearing heels, but hers are sky
high compared to mine.

Picking up my drink, I take a sip and immediately
scrunch my face, it tastes like vinegar mixed with gasoline
that's been poured through a dirty boot...hence, why it's
the free glass upon arrival tonight, I'm guessing.

Grabbing the bartender's attention, I order myself a
cosmo, and luckily for me, Embry is serving. He makes
THE best cocktails—his espresso martinis are to die for.

A few glorious minutes later, I have a cosmo in hand.
After the first sip, the vinegar/gasoline taste is gone and
it's replaced with the fruitiness of my cocktail.

Turning around, I lean against the bar and glance
around Prohibition, sighing in frustration. It looks like
Rarns and I are the only single ones here tonight, save for
a few fugly nerds in the corner.

"Ugh, why did I let you convince me to come?" I
whine to my possibly ex-best friend for making me come
out tonight...and really, really wishing I was back at home
in sweats and eating Cheetos.

"Because it's not acceptable to bring in the new year
by yourself, commiserating the demise of your relationship in sweats and eating Cheetos on the sofa. You need
to be looking fine and drinking wine."

"Oh, for fuck's sake, the rhyming's already started."

"And you wouldn't have me any other way," Rani
says, lifting her glass in a salute. She takes a sip of her
wine and winces like I did earlier.

"That wine is not so fine," I rhymingly tease back.

"Look at you rhyming, I'm so proud." She smiles sweetly and then grabs my cocktail and takes a sip, well a huge gulp, emptying my glass. Giving her the evil eye, she sweetly smiles, blows me a kiss, and then flags down Embry, ordering two more.

Shaking my head, I roll my eyes and laugh. That is one of the many things I love about my best friend, she always knows how to make me laugh, especially when it's inappropriate. Like at my grandparents' funeral earlier this year. He and Nanna were out for a walk last winter when a car hit a patch of black ice and killed them instantly. The only comfort I had in losing them was that they went together...and that's when Rani made me laugh, she made a joke about sex in heaven, and I burst out laughing. My laugh morphed into uncontrollable sobs. If it weren't for Kallen, Chels and Rani, I wouldn't have survived losing them. Kallen and my parents are what you'd call absentee parents, and thankfully, we had Nanna and Pops. They stepped in and looked after Kallen and me in a way our parents never could.

Embry places our cocktails down. "Thank you. Thank you. Thank you, Embry. You're my hero," Rarns informs him in an exaggerated tone.

"You just love me for my cocktails." He winks at her and wipes down the bar when I pick up my drink.

"Nah, it's your sexy ass," I nonchalantly throw back at him.

"You know it," he cheekily replies with another wink before spinning on his heel to saunter away. Making sure to add a butt shake my way. *Why are the gay ones always so awesome? Chad NOT included.* I miss working with him, I tended bar here when I was in college. Working with him was always fun...but drinking and giving him shit as a customer, is just as fun.

"If only you weren't gay," I quietly mumble as I pick up my cosmo. Taking a sip, I close my eyes and savor it.

"Drink up and let's dance," Rarns says, snapping my attention back to the present and away from my time tending bar here.

"I'm disappointed, no rhyme."

"There's still plenty of time, for me to rhyme," she replies with a wink, and then I notice that her drink is already gone. Seems my best friend plans to bring in the new year drunk as a skunk—damn it, now I'm rhyming. We, well I, finish my drink and just as I place the empty glass down, Rani grabs my hand and leads us out to the dance floor.

"Dance Monkey" by Tones and I begins to play. My body moves to the beat, and we jump around, letting loose. I have to admit, dancing with my bestie sure beats sitting on the sofa with my Cheetos, but I won't tell her that.

Opening my eyes, I stumble, because when I open them again, the sexiest of all sexy men is casually leaning against the bar staring directly at me. A sense of déjà vu washes over me, but I don't recall ever seeing this Adonis before. The dance floor is packed, but within the crowd, somehow, we've managed to connect. I stand frozen in the middle of the dance floor, and I take in the Adonis before me. Chiseled jaw. Sandy blond hair that I can imagine running my fingers through. He licks his bottom lip, and the light catches a silver ball on his tongue...and now I'm imagining his tongue licking me all over. Circling my nipple. Flicking my clit. Shit, I need to stop these dirty thoughts before I have an orgasm on the dance floor in Prohibition.

Tapping Rani on the shoulder, I nod to the restrooms. She's currently grinding up against some guy, and I dare say, she's found her New Year's kiss...and maybe more, going by the gyrations of their hips.

Squeezing between people, I head to the restrooms and luckily for me there's no line. I quickly pee and wash my hands. Before I head back out, I touch up my lip gloss and retighten my ponytail.

Heading back to the bar, Embry sees me and nods. "Fuck, he's gone," I whisper to myself as I lean my elbows on the bar top. My head begins swaying to the beat of the music.

My back is suddenly warm and my breath hitches in my throat but not in a scared way. If anything, my body is ablaze and turned on, like I was on the dance floor just moments ago.

Taking a deep breath, I spin around, and my eyes widen when I see who's behind me.

4

HUXLEY

LIKE A HEAT-SEEKING MISSILE, I find my mystery brunette when she's exiting the restroom hallway. My eyes track her movements over to the bar. Without her uttering a word, Embry nods at her and gets to making her cocktail.

Finishing my beer, I decide to go for it. I place one foot in front of the other and walk over to her. She's leaning against the bar, waiting for her drink, when I stop behind her. I'm close but not touching her. Close enough that I notice her shoulders hitch when she feels my presence.

She spins around and her eyes widen when she sees it's me. I also notice her gaze roam over me, but I can't fault her because I'm doing the same thing to her.

I open with, "Hi," grinning at her as the two-letter word passes through my lips. I could have pulled out a cheesy pickup line, but this woman deserves better than 'I ought to complain to Spotify for you not being named this week's hottest single' or 'I was wondering if you could tell me, if you're here, who's running Heaven?' and my favourite, 'I hope you know CPR, because you just took my breath away!'

"Hi, yourself," she replies, returning my grin. Up close she is even prettier than I first thought.

We stand here staring at one another, not saying anything. It's not awkward like some silences can be. It's like each of us is waiting for the other to break first.

At the same time, we both say our names. She laughs, and it's music to my ears. "I'm Kendall."

"Huxley," I offer. Leaning forward, I place a kiss on her cheek. Her skin is soft, and she smells like baby powder and something floral. It matches her style.

"Did you just sniff me?"

"No," I quickly refute. Internally scolding myself for being a creepy sniffer guy.

"I think you did."

"Well," I decide to go with honesty, "I did but not intentionally. I just so happened to breathe as I leaned in to kiss you."

"Likely story, Huxley Who-Likes-to-Sniff-Women-When-He-Kisses-Them-Hello."

Once again, we fall silent and stare at one another. The stare off this time is broken when Embry places her cocktail on the bar. "Here you go, Kendall." Then he looks to me. "Another beer, Hux?"

"Please," I reply with a nod, but my eyes are locked on Kendall. "What are you drinking this evening?"

She picks her drink up and raises it toward me. "Cosmos."

Embry passes me another beer, and as I reach over to

grab it, I once again breathe in and smell her. My eyes widen when I realize what I just did.

"Again?" she teases.

"I can't help breathing around you."

"Mmmhmpf," she teases.

She wraps her lips around the straw in her drink and sips. My mind goes to those delectable lips wrapped around my dick, and I have a feeling she's thinking the same thing because her eyes drop to my crotch. She lifts her gaze back up and I notice that her cheeks are now a lovely shade of 'aroused pink'.

"Were you just looking at my junk?"

"No," she snaps. "I was...I was enjoying my drink."

"Okay, I'll not believe that, and you can keep lying to yourself." She rolls her eyes at me, and I can't help but laugh. "So, Kendall Who-Wasn't-Looking-at-my-Junk, what do you do?"

"I'm the marketing director for Luxe here in Vancouver."

"That's cool."

"And what do you do, Huxley Who-Wasn't-Sniffing-Me-Earlier?"

I smile at the playful banter happening between us, I haven't felt this comfortable with someone in a long time. Maybe I don't need Hayd as my wingman after all? "I'm a rig worker up in Alberta, but soon I'm moving to Kiti-mat, somewhere a bit closer to home."

"Sounds dangerous."

"It can be at times." My mind drifts back to the explosion last year that nearly took Hayden's life. Ever since then, the thrill of the job hasn't been there, but the money is too good to refuse, and truth be told, I love the work.

"Hey, you okay?"

"Yeah, I'm fine. Just thinking about work."

"On New Year's Eve?"

"What can I say?" I offer with a shrug. "Chelsea Dagger" by the Fratellis begins to play and I notice Kendall begins to sway. "Kendall, would you like to dance?"

"Sure," she replies with a nod.

Plucking the straw out of her drink, she licks the end of it and then chugs back the rest of her cocktail. Placing the empty glass on the bar top, she looks to me and raises her eyebrows nodding toward my unfinished beer. Lifting the bottle to my mouth, I drink the remaining liquid and place the empty bottle down next to her glass. Offering her my hand, she places her palm in mine, and I lead us out to the dance floor.

We squeeze through and I find a spot in the middle. Turning to face her, I tug on her hand, and she falls into me. Her hands land on my chest and I slide mine around her waist, pulling her closer. We are roughly the same height, so our eyes are locked steadfastly on one another. I hold her hand on my chest and gently grip it in mine. She slides her other around my waist, and we begin to sway to the music, not even remotely in sync with the beat, but neither of us seems to care.

Our eyes are locked on one another.

Everyone around me fades away.

It's just Kendall and me.

She leans forward and I think she's going to kiss me,

but instead, she turns her head at the last minute and rests it on my shoulder. Gliding my hand up her back, I hold her just under her armpits. My fingertips grazing the side of her boob, she shivers in my arms and a smile graces my face at her reaction.

The song has changed, but I can't tell you what it changed to because I'm focused on the woman in my arms. Someone bumps into us and breaks the spell that fell upon us.

She lifts her head from my shoulder and stares at me, we are under a new spell now. The air around us thickens. My heart begins to race. She leans forward and this time, I'm sure she's going to kiss me. Her lips are millimeters from mine when someone pulls on her arm, taking her away from me and our kiss.

"Uhh ah, babe, save the smooching for midnight." I notice it's the friend who she was dancing with before.

Kendall shakes her head. "Did I see you, not five minutes ago, making out with..." She nods toward the guy who she was mauling earlier.

"Yeah, but that's different."

"Oh yeah, and how so, Rarns?"

She shrugs, turns away from us, and starts making out with said guy

Kendal faces me again. "So, that's my best friend, Rani."

"She seems..." I don't know so I just shrug.

"Yep, that's about right," Kendall says with a giggle, then she looks intently at me. "So, should we wait 'til midnight for that kiss? Or should we just do it now?"

"Maybe we should kiss now and get some practice in for midnight?" I offer as a suggestion.

"I like your style, Huxley I-Don't-Know-What-Your-Last-Name-Is. I think it's a great plan."

"Me too, Kendall I-Don't-Know-What-Your-Last-Name-Is."

Lifting my hands, I grip her cheeks in my palms and press my lips to hers. An electrical current zaps through my lips, igniting every nerve ending in my body. Never have I had a reaction like this to a kiss before.

Her tongue sweeps into my mouth, and I swallow back a moan, that is until I hear a sexy moan come from her. All bets are off now. I slide my hand around the back of her neck and hold her closer as I continue to assault her mouth with my tongue.

We've stepped up from kissing to tongue fucking, it's not really appropriate for the middle of a bar but I don't give a shit. I could die right now, and I'd die a fucking happy man.

Kendall breaks the connection between us. "Wow," she breathlessly utters against my lips.

"Wow indeed," I reply. "I think we should practice some more, maybe like seven times."

"Seven kisses, huh?"

"Yep...just to make sure we get it right for midnight."

"Well, practice does make perfect."

Not giving her a chance to change her mind, I press my lips to hers for another, searing, out-of-this-world kiss.

I want to kiss this woman forever.

One kiss just isn't enough.

5

KENDALL

AND THAT'S what we do, we lock lips again and this time it's even more mind-blowing than the one just before. *How is that possible?* I've kissed a few guys in my time, but never have they been as amazing as kissing Huxley. He's totally helping me forget all about Chad and Tad.

Even his name is sexy. Huxley, Hux...now I'm imagining how it will sound as I scream his name through a climax.

He slips his tongue into my mouth again; the stud strokes my tongue, and I moan into our kiss. I've never kissed a guy with a tongue piercing before, and I have to say, best kisses ever.

"Get a room, you skank," Rani says, hip bumping me, pulling me away from Huxley and his delectable kisses.

"Says the one who was mounting..." I look to the guy behind her and realize it wasn't the guy from earlier. Now who's the skank? "...him a few moments ago." I go with that to be safe.

She just shrugs and drags the guy into her arms on the dance floor and begins to grind up on him again. Rani is a very promiscuous girl, but she has a heart of gold and she's no pushover.

Looking back to Huxley, I'm panting and actually thankful for the interruption, because I was two point five seconds away from mounting him right here in the middle of the dance floor. That's a Rani thing and as much as I love my bestie, that's not me.

He flicks his head toward the bar, and I nod. He takes my hand in his, lacing our fingers together, and leads me off the dance floor. As we approach, he lifts his hand to Embry and indicates two more. To which he nods and goes about getting our drinks.

"So, you come here often?" he asks me, and as soon as the words leave his mouth, he scrunches his face in an 'Oh, my god, I did not just say that' kind of way, and I laugh.

"That line work often?"

"I don't know, I'll let you know after midnight."

"Smooth, real smooth."

"You ain't seen nothin' yet, baby."

Oh, my fucking god, this man...I have no words. Right now, I'm ever so grateful that Rarns made me come out tonight because I'm having a great time with Huxley. Not only is he a fantabulous kisser but we get along great. Sure, we haven't spoken much but when we have, it hasn't felt like other 'wham-bam-thank-you-ma'am' hook-ups that I've had before.

"So, when do you head back to work?" I ask him, just as Embry places our drinks down.

"Tomorrow," he dejectedly says.

"You're not excited about it?"

"Yes. No. I don't know."

"Wanna talk about it?"

"Yes. No. I don't know," he repeats again. "It's just, I love what I do, but now, now it feels like it's the same thing over and over."

"Like *Groundhog Day*?"

"Kinda, yeah."

"What's changed?" He thinks about my question, and when he looks up, he's staring out on the dance floor. Looking over my shoulder, I see him staring at a couple, who are clearly very much in love, and I start to wonder if he's pining for her.

He notices my expression change, he reaches over and squeezes my hand, that one touch reassures me that he's here for me. "That's my best friend, Hayden, and his wife. He was with me in an explosion last year and everything changed after that. He met Bryce, they had a whirlwind romance and eloped. He got his happily ever after, and me, I'm still plodding along. I guess..."

"You guess that now he's moved on, you should too and because you haven't, you feel lost and alone, as such."

He nods. "Yeah, pretty much. How'd you know?"

"Because I understand where you're coming from. Earlier this year, I was in Hawaii, helping out at our new hotel there. I know this couple, and after a humongous debacle, they got their HEA." He scrunches his eyes in confusion. "Let me explain, my friend and the CEO had a moment while on vacation once. They lost contact and finally met again. Secrets were kept, and of course, secrets always come out. Especially when a vindictive ex and the brother from hell want to see you fall off your pedestal, but that's beside the point. Seven years later, they got their happily ever after. I'm not ashamed to admit that I'm envious of them but life isn't always sunshine, roses, and birds singing like in fairy tales. I was beginning to think that happily ever afters and fairy tales aren't in the cards for me, well, until tonight that is."

We stare at one another and process my words. They were deeper than I intended, but the words just poured out once I opened my mouth. We continue to gaze at one another and a feeling of déjà vu washes over me again.

"Have we met before?" I ask him.

Huxley lifts his hand and cups my cheek in his palm. "I don't think so because I'm sure I would remember you."

That déjà vu feeling disappears and another feeling takes over, a feeling that I've never felt before with a guy. "Huxley, I think we were meant to meet each other tonight. Like fate set it up and has a plan for us."

"Maybe, who knows? But what I do know is that I'm glad to have met you, Kendall I-Still-Don't-Know-What-Your-Last-Name-Is."

"Jones."

"Kendall Jones, it's been a pleasure meeting you, and I hope—"

"Ten," someone shouts from nearby.

Nine

Eight

Seven

Six

Five

Four

Three

Two

One

"Happy New Year!" everyone sings out.

Huxley slides his hand around my waist and pulls me into him. He slams his lips against mine in an all-encompassing kiss that leaves me breathless and light-headed.

"Happy New Year, Kendall Jones," he murmurs against my lips.

"Happy New Year, Huxley I-Don't-Know-What-Your-Last-Name-Is."

He says his last name, but with all the celebrations going on around us, I don't hear what he says, but his surname can come later because right now, I want another New year's kiss with Hux. Even though there are over one hundred people around us celebrating and bringing in the new year, my focus is on him and only him. Closing my eyes, I lean forward. I need to press my lips to his again. I'm addicted to his kisses, but I don't get my kiss because chaos erupts around us.

People are screaming.

Everyone running for safety.

The joyous occasion has turned into a bloodbath when someone stabs someone for kissing their girl at midnight.

Huxley and I get separated in the mayhem and lose each other in the bedlam. One minute I was in his arms, leaning in for another kiss, and the next we're separated when people start running and screaming for their lives.

Looking around, I yell his name, but I can't find him among the hordes of frantic people.

What started as an amazing night ended in chaos, death, and no way of contacting Huxley. See, no fairy tale happy ending for me. Happy fucking New Year to me!

6

KENDALL

...Valentine's Day

"REALLY, Rarns? Speed dating? On Valentine's Day?" Can this be any more cliche? Or better yet, shithouse? I thought my best friend knew me, I'm sooo not a speed dating kind of person, I'm a 'kiss some random, sexy dude on New Year's and be addicted after the most amazing out of this world kiss, only for chaos to erupt and I never see him again' kind of person.

"Yep," she matter-of-factly states as she steps over to my closet and pulls out my black skinny jeans and a red halter top that I totally forgot I had.

"Can't I just stay home, order Chinese, and watch Netflix?" I silently add, *and think about Huxley and the amazing New Year's we shared together until some asshole decided to stab another asshole and ruin my amazing New Year's. Assholes.*

"Put these on," she demands, ignoring my pleas. She

then pulls out my knee-high black suede boots. "And these." She looks to me and then scrunches her face, "And once you're dressed, I'll fix your hair. It looks like a bird's nest."

Looking to the mirror I shrug. "It's a messy bun."

"You got the mess part right. Now hurry up and get dressed, I want to get there early and scope out the talent."

"It's gonna be desperate and dateless dudes who live in their mom's basement and play *Minecraft* all day long."

"Ye of little faith. Now hop to it." She claps her hands excitedly. Exiting my bedroom, she singsongs, "I feel the need, the need for dating in speed."

"That doesn't even rhyme properly," I shout at her retreating form.

"Shut up and shower, my delicate flower."

Shaking my head, I sigh and roll my eyes at that one. Maybe a night out is what I need to get myself out of this funk. Picking up the clothes she chose for me, I walk into my en suite and turn the shower on.

As the water heats, I strip off and then scream when Rarns reappears and hands me a shot glass. There is only one Rani Murphy in the world—thank God for that—and she just so happens to be my best friend. I really am lucky to have her, especially when she brings me shots while I'm in the shower.

"Cheers, Big Ears." She raises her glass in salute and chugs it back.

Shaking my head at her rhyming cheers, I can't help the smirk that appears on my face. I stare back at my best friend, not bothering to cover up because, hello, we're girls and we all have the same bits.

"Cheers." I raise my glass in salute, and shoot the liquid back. My eyes widen and I cough as the liquid burns a fiery trail down my esophagus. I was expecting tequila, but nope, it was vodka. "Ugh, really?" I protest, slamming the empty glass down on the vanity.

"Well, you had no tequila, and I didn't think you'd want to shoot cooking sherry, so I went with vodka, plus it counts as one serving of veggies since it's made from potatoes. Those lil' things are such versatile fuckers. Vodka. French fries. Mash. Poutine. Chips. All those other veggies are such slackers."

"As much as I'm loving this Potato 101 lesson, you mind fucking off so I can get ready?"

"So now you dooooo want to go out?" she sasses. Flipping her the bird, I turn my back on her and hop into the shower.

As I lather up the shampoo in my hair, I can hear her still mumbling to herself about potatoes and their versatility. A laugh escapes me and now I really want poutine.

I poke my head out, "Dammit, bitch, now I want poutine."

"Hurry up. Then we can get there early and get our poutine on while we wait to get our speed on."

"Your rhyming is really shitty tonight, Rarns."

"I know, what's up with that?"

"Maybe you finally subconsciously realize that it's fucking stupid and now you'll just speak like a normal human being."

"Normal is ugh, so normal."

"Funny that normal would be normal. Can you pass me my hair towel?"

She hands it to me, and I wrap my hair up. Then I wash my body and quickly shave my legs. Not that I'm planning on meeting anyone tonight, but skinny jeans with shaved legs is an amazing feeling. It's like climbing into bed with fresh, clean linens.

I'm sitting cross-legged in front of my mirror and applying my makeup while my bestie does my hair, perks of having a hairdresser as your best friend.

With my hair and makeup on point, I get dressed into the outfit she picked out for me. Zipping up my boots, I stand up and look at myself in the mirror, earning myself a whistle from Rarns.

"If I liked pussy, I'd totally do you," she tells me as she steps into my room from her shower. Turning around, I take her in, she's only in a strapless bra and panties.

"Bit underdressed, don't you think?"

"If it wasn't negative a billion outside and I wouldn't get arrested, I'd totally go out like this. The world needs to see these killer curves and my girls." She cups her boobs and then slips into a navy blue, skin-tight boob-tube dress.

"With that dress, you may as well be naked. It's like a second skin."

"I know, right?" She winks and pulls on boots with a heel that adds five inches to her already six-foot frame.

"How the hell do you walk in heels that high?"

"Says the one wearing boots with heels."

"My heels are half your size," I throw back at her. Sure, I love heels—just like Carrie Bradshaw in *Sex and the City*—but they need to be of a normal height—high enough to walk like a sexy confident woman, but not so high that I'm a wobbling mess.

She shrugs at me, and within three seconds, her hair is done in a messy updo that looks like she spent hours getting it just right. "You amaze me when you do that."

"Do what?" she questions, swiping on her signature red lipstick.

"That." I circle my finger up and down her body. "I took like an hour, WITH help from you on my hair, and you, you're ready and smokin' hot in a quarter of that time."

"Well, when you're naturally beautiful like me, it's easy peasy lemon squeezy."

"So, you're saying I'm fugly?"

"No, Jim Jarlath from tenth grade is fugly. You are hot. We, well me, just enhanced your hotness tonight."

Jim Jarlath, I haven't thought of him in years. He wasn't the most attractive-looking person, but it was his personality that really made him fugly.

"Enhanced my hotness, really?"

"Really, really. Now, let's get you some poutine and me a fella to keep me warm tonight."

Ugh, the speed dating thing, I totally forgot about that. "How about we just have a girls' night?"

"Nope, I paid fifty bucks each for these tickets. We are going to go speed dating and drink free bubbly and find someone to go mating."

Shaking my head, I grab my purse and head out for a night that turns out not quite how I expected.

7

HUXLEY

"TELL me again why we're here?" I ask Danny, Bryce's gay co-worker, who over the time that Bryce and Hayd have been together has become a good friend of mine too.

"Because it's Valentine's Day."

"So, because it's Valentine's Day, you're dragging me to a speed dating event?"

"Yep," he says, letting the 'p' pop.

"You do know that I'm not gay and this is a gay speed dating event?"

"Oh yeah, I umm, ahh, I didn't really think of that."

Tonight is going to be utter horseshit. When Danny first suggested speed dating, I thought it would be fun. However, when we arrived and I saw the clientele, I realized that this would, in fact, NOT be fun for me since I like women and not men.

However, the evening takes a pleasant turn when the door swings open and I see the last person I expected to see walk in. My eyes rake over her body, and fuck, she's just as gorgeous as I remembered.

She finally looks up and like a scene from a cheesy RomCom, she stops mid-step. Our gaze connects. Everything around us fades away.

On autopilot, I walk over to her. "Kendall."

"Huxley." My name has never sounded so sexy passing through anyone's lips.

"Well, this is a surprise," her friend, Rani, if I remember correctly says. "I'll get us drinks."

"What are you doing here?" I ask her.

"Speed dating, Rarns dragged me here."

"You do realize this is a gay men's speed dating event." Her eyes widen and then she looks around the room.

"Oh fuckballs, I'm gonna kill her."

"Orrrrr," I suggest, "you can spend the evening with me."

She stares at me and nods. "I think I'd like that, plus I don't look good in orange."

Before my brain has a chance to tell my mouth to stop, I blurt out. "I think you'd look beautiful in orange."

She stares at me, and her lips lift into a small grin. Clearly, I wasn't too cheesy after all, and then once again my mouth moves without permission from my brain. "I've been thinking about you since New Year's."

"Me too," she lowers her gaze and quietly whispers, "I hate that the evening ended how it did."

"Crazy ending to the evening, that's for sure...and not how I was hoping it would end."

She lifts her gaze back to mine. "Not how I wanted it to end either." She bites her lip. "So, how about we grab a drink and hide out at a table in the back?"

"I'd like that." Offering her my elbow, she slides her arm through, and we walk toward the bar.

Her friend walks past and singsongs, "Don't do anything I wouldn't do." Before either of us can reply, she takes her seat and joins in the speed dating.

"What'll it be?" the chick behind the bar asks us.

"Beer," we both say at the same time. Kendall giggles and I find myself smiling.

"Two Canadians," I tell the bar lady.

"So, Kendall Jones—"

"You remember my last name?"

"I remember everything about you, Kendall Jones." *Oh.My.God, can I be any cornier?* I internally berate myself, but from the smile on her gorgeous face, maybe I'm not as corny as I think. "What have you been up to since New Year's?"

"Work. Eat. Sleep. Repeat. And you?"

"Work. Sleep. Dream about you. Repeat."

"No eating?" she teases.

"Okay, let me rephrase. Work. Think about you. Eat. Think about you. Sleep. Dream about you. Repeat... thinking about you."

"Wow, you've done a lot of thinking lately...and for the record, I've thought about you a lot too, not in a stalkery way, just in a..." But she doesn't finish and tell me in what way she was thinking about me.

"Thinking about me, how?"

"You know," she nonchalantly replies with a shrug of her shoulder.

Our beers are placed on the bar top, she picks hers up and takes a sip. Never has watching someone drink a beer before been so...erotic. "I have a feeling, I was thinking about you how you were thinking about me, going by the look in your eyes right now."

"Oh yeah, and what look is that?"

"Like you want to kiss me again."

"One kiss definitely isn't enough when it comes to you, and I'm game if you're game." I pick up my beer and bring it to my lips, but she reaches out and grabs my hand, halting me.

Grabbing my beer from my hand, she takes a sip, leans forward, and presses her lips to mine. Opening my mouth, she transfers the beer into mine and kisses me. Quickly I swallow and somehow don't choke as she continues to kiss me.

Sliding my hand around the back of her neck, I pull her closer and deepen the kiss. My tongue sweeps into her mouth, sliding around with hers. Pulling back, I rest my forehead on hers. "That is, by far, the best fucking way to drink a beer."

"I think so too, Huxley. Maybe we should do it again?"

"As tempting as that is, I think since we are in a public place, we need to stick to PGing the beer drinking."

"Fine," she relents. "But if the opportunity arises, we should totally drink our beer that way again."

"Deal."

We grab our beers and find a table in the back, away from the speed dating. I make a mental note that the next time I'm one-on-one with Danny, I will have to thank him for dragging me to this event. When I found out it was gay speed dating, I was pretty pissed, but since I ran into Kendall again, I'm not so pissed anymore.

"So apart from lots of thinking, what have you been up to?" she asks me.

"Working and working. I've been away since New Year's Day, and I've only had two days off in the last six weeks. We've been in the middle of a major shutdown, but I'm home for two weeks now."

"Wow, that's a lot of work."

"It's not normally so crazy but it was a major mainte-nance shutdown on one of the turbines."

"What would you normally work?"

"Two. Two. Two and four."

"What does that mean?"

"Two weeks at work. Two weeks off. Two more weeks at work and then four weeks off."

"Oh, that makes sense and is kind of a good schedule with the time off aspect."

"Yeah, it's a great schedule, allows for a lot of travel if I want."

"I bet. Where's your most favourite place you've been?"

"Seeing the northern lights in Rovaniemi."

"Where's that?"

"Lapland."

"Wow, sounds amazing."

"Words cannot describe it; it was phenomenal and majestic in every way. The glass igloos are pretty awesome and give you an unobstructed view all night long."

"I'd love to see it one day."

"I highly recommend it." And silently I add, *Maybe I can take you one day.* "So, what about you? Your most favourite destination?"

"You'd think working for a luxury hotel chain, I'd have visited some amazing locations, but alas, I have not —" Her eyes widen, and she jumps up. Her friend runs up to her, tears pouring down her cheeks. "What's wrong, Rarns?" she asks, engulfing her friend in a hug.

She blubbers something incoherently, and I have no clue what she just said, but clearly Kendall understands because her eyes widen farther, and she nods in understanding. She runs her hand soothingly up and down her friend's back. "It's going to be fine," she whispers. Her friend lifts her head and stares at her, shaking her head side to side.

"How? How do you know?" Rani cries.

Kendall grips her upper arms and looks her dead in the eyes. "Because Daddy Murph is a fighter, he IS a Murphy after all. I'll settle my tab and get you to Vancouver General."

She looks to me. "Sorry, I have to go." Before I have a chance to reply or offer to drive them, she's gone. She and her friend race out of the bar, leaving me alone...and again, without her digits.

8

HUXLEY

...St Patrick's Day

"COME ON, GUYS, LET'S GO," I shout to my soon-to-be ex—if he doesn't get his ass out here now—best friend and his wife. It's St. Patrick's Day, and for as long as I can remember, Hayden and I have attended the celebration here at Prohibition, and tonight will be no different. I don't care that he's married and Bryce is joining us tonight, the more the merrier I say.

"Coming," he yells, and it's accompanied by a giggle. I really hope he's not referring to THAT coming.

Finally, I hear footsteps echoing down the hallway and when I look up, I see Bryce. "Where's your husband?"

"Fixing his hair," she says with a smirk on her face, and I'm pretty sure his hair needs fixing because of her.

"Of course he is," I say, shaking my head, "You look lovely tonight, Bryce. Glowing even."

"Thanks," she replies with a sheepish smile. From the

look that washes over her, I'd bet my left nut that Mrs. Bowden is hiding something.

"Hayd, hurry up, dude, even your wife is ready."

"That's because she took over the bathroom," he complains, finally joining us.

"Don't blame the wife, now, let's go get our green drink on."

The Uber drops us off out front and waiting for us are Danny and Ruby, who are also joining us tonight. We all say our hellos and head inside. "A Good Heart" by Feargul Sharkey is playing, the girls and Danny grab a booth while Hayden and I head to the bar.

"What's up with you and Bryce? You're both acting weird."

"Nothing," he quickly snaps and turns away from me, and as soon as the bar dude reaches us, he orders. "A Fuzzy Leprechaun, a pitcher of beer, and a lime sherbet punch."

"Who's not drinking?" I question and then my eyes widen, "Is Bryce preggo?"

"Ummm, no," he replies, but I can tell he's lying so I give him the 'do I look dumb eye' and then he nods. "Yeah, she is, we just found out. You can't say anything."

"My lips are sealed." I mime zipping them. "But seriously, dude, congrats."

"Thanks, if I'm honest, I'm shitting my pants over it."

"Why?"

"I work away. How can I be a good dad if I'm away all the time? And what if I miss the birth? And what if something goes wrong and I'm away? I've already been on the end of being away when she was in the hospital, I can't do that again."

"Dude, she doesn't have a crazy-ass stalker stalking her anymore, and I'm sure that things with the baby will be grand, eh." I pause. "It's funny you mention it, I'm kinda over the away thing too."

"If we both leave, Troy will kick our asses."

"But what if we didn't leave? What if we propose something different?"

"Different like what?"

The music gets louder, Metallica's version of "Whiskey in the Jar" is booming, and everyone is singing along. "We can chat tomorrow. Meet me for lunch and we can discuss it."

"Deal." With our drinks in hand, we head over to the group. In the few minutes since we arrived, the place has filled up. Everyone is dressed in green, and the atmosphere is electric.

Taking a seat next to Danny, I pour three beers and hand them out. From the corner of my eye, I swear I see Kendall, but when I turn my head, I realize it's not her. I'm seeing her everywhere; I even swear I saw her on the rig. I'm going crazy. She has been at the forefront of my mind since Valentine's Day and every time I have a beer, I think of our beer kiss.

Maybe I need to hook up with someone else to get her out of my mind. What's the saying 'Best way to get over someone is to get UNDER someone else.' But that's the thing, I don't want to get over her. I want a chance with her but fate, the bitch, keeps intervening.

"What's up, Buttercup?" Bryce asks me, nudging my shoulder."

"Noth—"

"Don't bullshit me with saying nothing."

"Wow, those mom tendencies are strong already." Her eyes widen and then she looks to Hayden and gives him the eye. "Oops, I...umm...ahh, crap." I lean into her and whisper, "I won't say anything but I just wanna quickly say, I'm so happy for you both. This kid is gonna have amazing parents and a super awesome uncle."

"Thanks," she smiles at me, "to be honest, I'm freaking the fuck out but at the same time, I'm over the moon excited and I want to shout it from the rooftops."

"So do it."

She vehemently shakes her head. "Not 'til after twelve weeks. Too much can go wrong, and I don't want the pity looks. I got enough pity after the Dale thing; I don't want to feel like that again."

"No one pitied you, Bryce." She gives me the 'really' look. "Okay, a few douchewads did, but they don't count. Those that do count think you are strong and amazing and will be an amazing mom."

Her eyes well with tears, "Aww, thanks, Hux. And someday, you will make some girl lucky to call you her husband."

Not some girl, Kendall, I think to myself, if only I get the chance to see her again.

9

KENDALL

"ARE you thinking about the one that got away again?" Rarns asks me, again...for what feels like the millionth time in the last few months.

"No," I defensively reply, but my best friend knows me too well, even if we are chatting over the phone right now.

"I call bull poop, babe. You've been pining over this mystery guy since Valentine's Day," then she quietly adds, "and I went and ruined it for you."

"You did not ruin anything, Rarns. Daddy Murph needed us, and family always comes first."

"He could be your family though."

"After a few kisses, that's going a bit far." But there's a small part of me that thinks she could be right, there's something about Huxley I-Don't-Know-What-His-Last-Name-Is, and I'd love a chance with him...if only fate would stop being a bitch.

"Okay, it's St. Patrick's Day, therefore, we're going to Prohibition for the annual Green Party. You will pull on that sexy as fuck green halter dress and then you and I will drink green cocktails. Then, you're going to find another guy to smack lips with, effectively forgetting all about Amazing Kisses Boy."

"But—"

"No buts," she interrupts. And then I wait for it and on cue she adds, "Surely he wasn't that good of a kisser."

"They were the best kisses of my life, Rarns."

"Please," she scoffs, "no one is that good of a kisser. Well, except me that is."

There's no point in arguing so I just smile and drag my ass into a sitting position on my bed. "Fine," I relent.

"You better be looking divine."

I roll my eyes at her fine/divine rhyme. "Pick me up at seven."

"That's the spirit."

Hanging up, I walk into my kitchen and pour myself a glass of wine. With my glass in hand, I head back into my bedroom and do as she suggests. I pull on my green halter dress and then sit cross-legged in front of my mirror and do my makeup. I even attach sparkly green, fake eyelashes that even though they looked gaudy in the packet look amazing on and make my eyes pop.

As I'm swiping on my lipstick, I think about the kiss that got away and sigh. *Why didn't we exchange numbers?* That sentence has been floating around my head constantly. Maybe Rarns is right, maybe I need to find someone new.

Clearly fate has other plans for me, so I decide that, yes, tonight I will get my drink on and find someone to smooch. Then I can get over Hunky Huxley, once and for all.

The music is pumping at Prohibition by the time Rarns and I arrive. Metallica is singing about "Whiskey in a Jar." "I like the original so much better," Rarns whines.

Shaking my head, I take her hand and lead us to the bar. "Nope, I like this one."

"Of course you do."

She smiles at the bartender sweetly, but I deflate when I don't see Embry, no super amazing cocktails tonight. "Two fuzzy leprechauns, please." Then she looks back to me. "We will never ever agree on remakes, never ever ever."

"Probably not," I agree, then I cheekily add, "It's not my fault you've got shitty taste in music."

She sticks out her tongue at me.

"Such a comeback," I taunt her, earning myself another tongue stick.

With our cocktails in hand, we walk around trying to find an empty table or even a spot to stand. "Holy crap, it's busy here tonight."

"Crazy busy...at least it should be easy for us to find a guy for you to smooch."

"Do I really have to smooch a random?"

"Yes, yes you do."

"Fine," I huff, "but he better be hot...and maybe have a tongue ring...and sandy blond hair. And muscles and hazel eyes."

"So, you want him to be Kisser Boy?"

"Yes," I cry. "I really want Kisser Boy. I'm not ready to move on yet."

"But what if Jason Statham walks through that door right this second?"

"Then my elbows are up, and I'll cut a bitch to get to him."

"Your crush on him is something epic."

"Umm, hello, if Nick Bateman waltzed in here, you'd do the same."

"Yes. Yes, I would." She lets out a dreamy sigh. "Dammit, girl, now my panties are all wet thinking about him."

"TMI, Rarns. TMI."

She shrugs at me and finishes her drink. "Your shout."

"Laaaaaaaaa," I singsong loudly and then laugh at my lame-ass joke.

"Not the shout I'm referring to and you know it." She shoves her empty glass at me. "Cocktail me now, brown cow," she says now brown cow in a posh, haughty way.

"Did you watch *The Nanny* tonight?"

"Yeah, I did. I loved that show. Drinks. Now. Go."

"Wow, you're bossy tonight."

She sticks her tongue out at me. "One day when you do that, I'm gonna pull on your tongue."

"You wouldn't dare," she replies in disgust.

"Try me."

Turning on my heel, I walk toward the bar to get more drinks. Placing my order, I turn around and lean against the bar. Looking around, I smile when I realize that everyone is dressed in green. And thinking about green has me thinking about Huxley and his gorgeous hazel eyes, they are a unique shade of hazel.

Someone taps my shoulder, and I look over to see my drinks on the bar. "Thanks," I say and hand over my card.

A lady slips in next to me, and she sighs just as I take a sip and also sigh. The tang of the pineapple and peach schnapps dances an Irish jig on my tongue.

"God, that looks good," she dreamily says, looking at the drink in my hand.

"It is, you should order one."

"I will...in nine months' time." My gaze drops and I see nothing but a flat stomach. "I only just found out," she whispers.

"Well, congrats, and me being the awesome person I am, I'll be sure to have one, or five, of these in your honor."

"Why, thank you." She tips her head in thanks and then orders a pitcher of beer, a fuzzy leprechaun, and a virgin Shirley Temple.

"And I will also curse your name when I'm hungover as all hell tomorrow."

"And again, I thank you." She once again bows her head and when she lifts back up, we both giggle. "I'm Bryce."

"Kendall." I stretch out my hand, and she takes it in hers.

Her pitcher of beer and glasses are placed on the bar top, and the guy turns to make her cocktails. Looking at her and the drinks, I wonder how she'll carry them all back.

I should probably get back to Rarns, but I find myself enjoying her company so I stay. We look at one another and she studies me intently. It's kinda awkward but then she smiles, and the awkwardness dissipates. "Your lashes are on point, girl. I bought some but they looked like crap in the packet so I decided to forgo them."

"Would they happen to be Lash and Company?"

"Yes," she replies, letting the 's' hiss a little. Pointing to my eyes, I smirk at her. "No freakin' way."

"Yes, freakin' way."

"They look so much better on than in the packet."

"Well, think of it this way, you'll be set for St. Patrick's Day next year."

"Complete with my own lil' leprechaun."

"That will be too cute to see."

Finally, two cocktails are placed in front of Bryce, and that's when her face scrunches up when she realizes she has to carry all of it. "You want a hand with that?"

"Umm, ahh, yeah, I didn't really think this through when I offered to grab the next round." She pauses. "Do you mind?"

"Not at all. Will allow me to put my waitressing skills from college to good use." Bryce watches as I grab the pitcher and one cocktail in one hand, not spilling a drop. I pick up my drink in the other, "Where too?"

"That's freakin' amazing," she coos, shaking her head.

"I've still got it," I say with a wink. "Lead the way."

She grabs the glasses and remaining cocktail, and I follow her to a booth in the back. Along the way, I catch Rarn's eyes and nod to the drinks in my hand and mouth, 'Give me a sec.' She nods and turns her attention back to the guy beside her.

Placing the drinks down, Bryce looks to me. "Thank you again. Did you want to join us, Kendall?"

"Sure, let me just go grab my friend."

"Okay, see you soon."

Darting around people, I head over to Rani. Handing her her drink, I tell her I'm going to hang with Bryce. She nods but her attention is on the guy with her. Shaking my head, I head to the bar and order a drink and then I make my way over to Bryce, happy that I've made a new friend and I can stop thinking about Huxley...or so I thought.

10

HUXLEY

"I MADE A FRIEND AT THE BAR," Bryce informs Hayden when he and I rejoin them. We saw an old work colleague so we caught up for a chat.

"Oh yeah, an invisible one?" I tease since there's no one new in, or around, our booth.

She sticks her tongue out at me and picks up the pitcher of beer and begins to pour. "Hardy har har. She'll be here in a sec."

"How do you make friends everywhere we go?" Hayden asks, taking his beer from his wife.

"Just do," she nonchalantly replies. Handing me mine, she picks up her bright pink concoction and takes a sip.

"What's her name?" I ask, taking a sip of my beer, thankful that this year they didn't add green food colouring because that shit tasted like ass last year. While I wait for this mystery lady's name, I wonder if this chick will be the lady who will get my mind off Kendall.

"Kendall," she says, causing me to choke and spray beer everywhere.

"Did you say Kendall?"

"She sure did," a voice that I'd recognize anywhere says from behind me. Turning my head, I come face-to-face with the one who got away.

"Huxley," she says, her voice laced with shock when she realizes it's me.

"You two know each other?" Bryce asks us, her gaze flicking back and forth between us, and then her eyes widen when she makes the connection. "Oh.My.God, is this the kiss girl?"

"Kiss girl?" Kendall questions, her tone high and a little on edge.

All eyes are now on me, but mine are locked on Kendall's because I must be dreaming right now. Lifting my hand, I pinch her arm and she squeals, "Ouch, what the hell, Hux?"

"Just making sure I wasn't dreaming."

A hand smacks the back of my head. "Dick, you did not just pinch that girl," Hayden growls, shaking his head. "The least you could do is poke her." His eyes widen when he realizes what he just said. "Not poke her poke her but poke," he wiggles his index finger, "her."

"And you just keep digging that hole there, Hayd." Turning to Kendall, I smile. "You're really here."

"Really, really."

"Aaaaaw, she just Shrek'd him," Bryce coos, "I freakin' love that movie."

"Me too," Kendall replies, turning her attention from me to Bryce. "Donkey is the best."

In unison they say, "I need a hug." The two of them burst out laughing. When they've composed themselves, Bryce looks to me. "She's a keeper, Westie."

I agree, I silently think to myself and when I look up again, all eyes are on me. "What?"

"Do you agree she's a keeper?" Bryce presses me again.

"Way to put a guy on the spot." From the corner of my eye, I see Kendall's face deflate so I quickly tack on, "And to answer your question, I do think that." She lifts her gaze to mine and she smiles. "Would you like to dance, Kendall?"

"I think I'd like that," she shyly replies.

Placing my beer down, I offer her my hand. She looks down at it and then places her palm in mine. Like each time we touch, a spark jolts between us, cementing once again that the two of us do have a connection.

With her hand in mine, we walk toward the dance floor.

My heart is pounding in time to the bass pumping through the speakers. Like the night we met, "Chelsea Dagger" by The Fratellis is playing. "We danced to this song on New Year's," I inform her as I spin her around and pull her into me.

"Yes, yes we did." She drapes her arms over my shoulders, and I rest my hands on her hips. We sway to the beat, our eyes locked on one another. "We should..."

"Should what?"

She drops her gaze and bites her bottom lip. Lifting my hand, I place my finger under her chin and lift. "We should what, Kendall?"

"Kiss again," she quietly murmurs.

"We should," I matter-of-factly state and before she has time to change her mind, I grip her cheeks in my palms, lean forward, and press my lips to hers. She covers my hands with hers and kisses me back.

Breaking the connection, we stare at one another. Lowering my hands to her waist, I rest them on her hips, and she drapes hers back over my shoulders. Our bodies sway to the music, but I remain focused on her. "You are a phenomenal kisser, Kendall Jones."

"You still remember my last name?"

"I remember everything about you, but I think I need a reminder on one thing."

"Oh yeah, and what's that?"

"This." Leaning forward, I press my lips to her again. Her mouth opens in shock, and I take the opportunity to slip my tongue back into her mouth.

Pulling back, I rest my forehead against hers and smirk. "Yep, just as I remember."

"Just as you remember what?"

"Kissing you is the best thing ever."

"So, Huxley..." she stops and looks quizzically at me. "What's your last name?"

"Weston. Huxley Weston."

"Bringing out your inner Bond I see." I shrug at her.

We stare at one another, and a feeling of being home washes over me. Is this woman 'the one'? or am I reading into things because of all the serendipitous moments? Whatever it is, I'm going to enjoy my time with her.

"What were you going to say before I went all Weston. Huxley Weston, on you."

"Right, if I remember correctly, on New Year's you needed seven to be sure."

"I definitely don't need seven, but I will happily take seven kisses."

A smile graces her face. Her tongue darts out and she licks her bottom lip. "Come with me," she pants. She takes my hand in hers and pulls me across the dance floor, through the crowd, and down the corridor to the restrooms. I'm a little confused right now, that is until she pulls me into a room at the end. The door closes behind us and she flips the lock.

Looking around, I see a sofa and a row of lockers. "Staff room?" I voice.

She nods. "I tended bar here in college. It's probably not okay, but I just needed..."

"Needed what?" I feel like I'm questioning everything at the moment, but so far, I have liked the answer to each question and since we're now locked in a private room together, I think I'll like the answer again.

"Some quiet with you." She pauses. "Fate keeps interrupting us and I'm hoping that if it's just the two of us, fate can't fuck it up for the third time."

"Yes, fate seems to be a moody bitch at the moment when it comes to us."

"Moody is one way of putting it." She swallows deeply. "I'm glad she intervened this time though because it's good to see you again."

"Anytime I see you it's good." Man, can I be any cheesier, this woman is bringing out my inner cheese tonight.

"And I think tonight, we will take that good and turn it into phenomenal."

"Phenomenal, huh?" She nods. "And how do we go about that?"

She bites her lip and stares at me. "Well, for starters, I think you should kiss me again."

I don't give her a chance to add on anymore, I reach out and grab her wrist. Pulling her into me, I cover her mouth with mine and I do exactly as she requested. I kiss her. I kiss her like she's never been kissed before.

She presses on my chest and walks me backward. The back of my legs hit the sofa and she pushes me. I fall to the sofa and stare up at her. Her cheeks are flushed, and she has never looked more beautiful. She rests her knee on the cushion beside my leg and throws her other leg over. The hem of her dress rises, but as if fate is taunting me, it doesn't rise all the way up. Straddling me, she cups my cheeks in her palms and kisses me again.

Running my hands up her back, I pull her as close to me as possible. Her breasts press against my chest, and even through the material of our clothes, it feels amazing. I can only imagine what this will feel like with nothing between us.

Sliding my hands down to her ass, I grip her cheeks in my palms and massage. She swivels her hips, and the movement causes my cock to harden between us. My dick is painfully pressing against my zipper, but the feeling of her rubbing herself on me makes the pain fade away.

With my hand on her ass, I lift her up and gently lower

her to her back on the sofa. Cocooning her underneath my body, I kiss down her neck. Peppering kisses gently on her skin, down the neckline of her halter dress. She moans in delight when I cup her boob in the palm of my hand.

Gently massaging her plump mound, she presses her chest up into my palm. Kissing across her chest, I push the material out of the way, baring her breast. Her nipple hardens when the cool air of the staff room hits. Taking the taut peak into my mouth, I gently suck.

"Huxley," she moans my name.

"Harder," she breathlessly begs.

"Yes," she mewls, running her fingers through my hair. "Yes. Yes. Yes."

I suck harder on her nipple, gently biting the tip. She runs her fingers through my hair, scratching her nails along my scalp, pushing me farther into her. I begin to massage her other breast. Unintelligible words slip from her mouth, and I smile as I continue to suck and fondle her tits.

Kissing back up toward her mouth, I pull my lips from her body. Her eyes open from the lack of contact, she breathlessly stares up at me. Reaching up, she cups my cheek in her palm. "Do you wanna get out of here?"

11

KENDALL

I'M NEVER FORWARD like this, but this is the third time I've seen Huxley and this time, I *will* get an orgasm from him. However, I have to admit that ten more seconds of him giving the girls attention like that and I totally would have orgasmed. Now, I'm really hoping that since I offered for us to go back to my place, I WILL get said orgasm. Well, as long as he agrees to come home with me...but then again, I do have fingers and an amazing collection of battery-operated objects, thanks to my sexy, fantasy nights toy collection.

The tongue on this man is unbelievable. Kissing him and having that piercing in my mouth is amazing, but when he sucked on my boob, holy hell. That little silver ball scraping over my sensitive flesh is everything. I cannot wait to feel it between my thighs, but I refuse to do that in the staff room here at Prohibition. Making out and almost coming is acceptable, but anything more is just tacky.

It feels like an eternity before he gives me his answer. "I'd fucking love to go home with you, Kendall Jones."

He slams his lips to mine, kissing the ever-loving shit out of me. "Kissing you is amazing, Hux," I breathlessly whisper against his lips.

"You know what's even better?"

"What?" I ask because right now, my brain isn't functioning to full capacity. I'm in a Huxley haze and I have to say, I love it.

"Naked kissing. Naked kissing is so much better."

"Naked kissing," I repeat, "I think I like the sound of that."

"Well then, what do you say, wanna get out of here and try naked kissing with me?"

"Yes." I nod. "Yes, I do."

"Good, then let's go."

He pushes himself up to hop off, but I wrap my arms around his neck, holding him above me. "In a minute. Huxley, I need to kiss you again because I don't trust that fate won't fuck this up between us."

"I'm sure I can oblige you with another quick kiss, Kendall, because I have to say, kissing you is fast becoming a favourite hobby of mine."

"Mine too, Hux, mine too. Now less talking and more kissing."

"Yes, ma'am."

Quick and Huxley do not go together in a sentence, because our quick kiss turns into a fifteen-minute, full-on make-out session that also includes another amazing boob kiss and grope.

Righting our clothes, Huxley orders an Uber and then we exit the staff room. He laces his fingers with mine, and we head over to his friends. We say our good-byes and walk away from them to find Rarns so I can say goodbye to her. I find Rarns on the dance floor and nod to Hux and the door. She raises her eyebrows suggestively, smiles her megawatt smile, mimics calling with her thumb and pinkie stretched apart, and she shakes as she holds it to her ear.

Nodding, I blow her a kiss and then Huxley and I exit Prohibition.

We step outside and I immediately start to shiver. There's still a chill in the air, but that chill quickly disappears when Huxley hugs me from behind as we wait for our ride to arrive.

Seems fate is on our side tonight because the car arrives quickly, and we jump in. The warm air blowing from the heater is bliss, but when Hux rests his palm on my thigh and gently rubs his thumb back and forth, my body temperature skyrockets and my blood begins to simmer.

Looking over at him, I watch him intently as the car drives us toward my place. He really is a good-looking guy. He must feel me staring because he turns his head and stares back at me.

Lifting his hand, he cups my cheek. "You really are beautiful."

A laugh erupts, and I shake my head. "I was just thinking the same thing about you."

"I'd more describe myself as ruggedly handsome."

"That works too," I agree. I'm about to lean in for another kiss when the car comes to a stop. Looking up, I notice that we're at my place already. I was so engrossed in Huxley that I didn't even realize where we were.

Huxley climbs out first, and I scoot across the back seat. He offers me his hand and escorts me out of the car. Closing the door, I lace my fingers with his, and we walk up the path toward the front doors of my building.

All of a sudden, butterflies take flight in my stomach. I can't remember the last time I was nervous when I brought a guy home. Actually, I can't remember the last time I brought a guy home, period. I normally suggest their place; stranger danger and all that, but when it comes to Huxley Weston, I feel safe. Which is odd, considering I know jack-all about him. But I get this vibe from him, and it makes me feel safe and cherished. I know he won't hurt me or stalk me. Well, I hope I'm right. I hope I'm not in some kissing fog and under his kissing spell.

I laugh at that thought.

"What's so funny?"

"Nothing," I tell him as I unlock the door to my building. We step into the lobby and walk over to the elevators. Fate is once again on our side—I think she's making up for the New Year's and V-Day mishaps—and they open immediately. It shocks me because these are the slowest elevators in the history of elevators. Some days, it's quicker to take the stairs...and I live on the seventh floor.

Stepping into the car, I press the button for seven. The doors begin to close...slowly...ever so slowly. Huxley and I stare silently at the doors and finally, after a billion years, they close and then we wait...wait for the elevator to whisk us up to my floor.

"Sooo," he voices, breaking the silence, "how you doin?"

A laugh breaks free and I snort. Embarrassed at my snort, I cover my face and continue to giggle into my palm. Why? Why did I have to snort right now? He must think I'm a freak.

He wraps his hands around my wrists and pulls them away from my face. Lifting my gaze, I stare into his gorgeous green eyes. "Don't hide your beautiful face from me."

"I'm so embarrassed that I snorted."

"Don't be, some people snort when they laugh. Some sound like a hyena and some sound like a witch cackling, while some—"

Pressing my finger to his lip, I stop him. "I get it, laughs are all different."

We stare at one another with my finger pressed to his lips. Dropping my gaze, I stare at my finger on his lips, I should remove it but I can't, well, I don't want to. It's only my finger, but I like touching him.

He opens his mouth and sucks my fingertip into it. The sensation sends a jolt of electricity through my body, causing my clit to tingle and buzz. A moan slips out, and he smiles around my fingertip.

He walks me backward until my back hits the elevator wall. He pulls my finger out of his mouth and then ever so slowly—but faster than the elevator—he slides his hands down my body, brushing the edges of my breasts before resting on my hips. He squeezes gently, causing another moan to slip free.

Leaning forward, he presses his lips to mine, but before we can begin kissing, the elevator doors finally open. Kissblocked by the elevator; seems bitchy fate is back.

Placing a quick kiss on his cheek, I grab his hand and pull him out of the elevator. Walking down the hallway to my door, I dig in my clutch for my keys, but it takes longer than it should because Huxley is distracting me, kissing and nipping my skin around my ear. Leaning my head back and to the side, I give him full access to my neck.

Reaching around me, he slips his hands under the material of my dress and cups my boobs, gently massaging. Again, my clit jolts to life and I moan. I begin to grind my ass against his crotch, his cock thickening with each swivel of my hips. I'm ready to turn around and hump him in the hallway, but I don't think old Mrs. Clarke across the hall wants to see that.

"Let me get this door unlocked," I breathlessly pant, "and..." But I drift off because he bites my earlobe and I become a pile of goo in his arms. I've never reacted to a guy like this before. Huxley can play my body like a well-trained musician. And I don't mind at all. I just wish we were inside and naked.

Finally, I find my key and somehow manage to get it into the lock, turn it, and open my door. With our bodies fused together, we step into my apartment. He kicks the door closed behind him, spins us and presses me into the wood, my back to his front. I can feel his breath on my neck. "Kendall, babe, I'm two point five seconds away from ripping this sexy as fuck dress off your body and devouring you."

Looking over my shoulder, I pant, "Do it."

12

HUXLEY

THOSE TWO WORDS are magic to my ears.

Sliding my hand out of her dress, I reach for the zipper on the side and lower it down her body. She lifts the halter strap over her head and the material flutters to our feet, leaving her in nothing but a barely-there G-string and her sexy as fuck heels.

Taking a step back, my gaze runs down her back to her ass and I groan, "Fuck me, Kendall, you are exquisite." She looks over her shoulder at me and spins around, giving me a front view. "Fuuuuck, you are even more stunning from the front."

Stepping back to her, I slam my lips against hers—I love kissing this woman—one kiss was never going to be enough. Gripping her ass, I pull her against my body and press my tongue into her mouth. She opens and accepts, twirling hers around the stud in mine.

"Please," she murmurs against my lips.

"Please, what?" I taunt her because I'm pretty sure

she wants what I want right now, but I need to hear her say it.

"Fuck me with your tongue."

Hmmmpfh, not what I was expecting her to say, but it's totally something I can happily get on board with.

"As you wish." Dropping to my knees, I pull her to me. Gripping her thighs, just under her ass, I press my face into her mound and inhale. Her panties are soaked. Breathing in deeply, I smell her arousal. "Fuuuuck, you smell delicious. Let's see if you taste as delicious." Running my tongue over the silky material, I groan. I don't know if I'm torturing myself or her but either way, I need to taste more.

Gripping the side of her underwear, I quickly tug the material down her legs, exposing her bare, glistening pussy to me. Sliding my tongue between her folds, I lick up and down her slit, sucking on her clit when I reach the top.

Kendall runs her fingers through my hair, tugging the strands when I gently bite her clit. "Huuuuuuxley," she moans.

Slipping a finger in, she unabashedly moans, pushing herself onto my face farther. Inserting another finger, I continue to lick, suck, and finger fuck her, and she continues to hold my head captive between her thighs. It's hard to breathe right now but if I died from suffocation, it would be the most epic way to die.

Out of nowhere she screeches, "I'm coming."

No sooner does she finish yelling that, her body stiffens, and my face is drenched with her release. I lick and suck as much as I can, but there's a lot. I don't think I've ever seen a woman climax this much before.

Her body relaxes and she falls into me, pushing me backward, I land on my back with an 'uff.' Kendall is draped on top of me, breathing heavily. She lifts her head and stares at me, "I...I don't think I've ever come that hard from head before. You, Huxley Weston, have a magical tongue." *Chad who?*

No one has ever said that to me before, and I find myself grinning. "You are very welcome, Kendall Jones." Cupping her cheek, I run my thumb along her jawbone. "As much as I'm loving the feeling of your naked body on mine, do you think we can sit up so I can move your clutch from behind my back? It isn't the most comfortable item to be lying on."

"Shit," she gasps, pushing herself off me and I immediately miss the feeling of her pressed against me. Offering me her hand, she pulls me up into a sitting position. She straddles my thighs and reaches around me to move her clutch. Her breasts press into my chest, and her pussy rubs against my cock. It's harder than steel right now, and her pressing against it is making it really uncomfortable. As if she's a mind reader, she shimmies back along my thighs. She flips open the button on my jeans and lowers the fly. I let out a contented moan at the impending freedom, but my moan soon turns from contentment to pleasure when she begins to stroke my cock.

"Kendall, babe, as much as that is amazing, I need to lose the jeans before I bust a nut. My cock is rock-hard and he's not happy being confined in my jeans right now."

"Well, we can't have that now, can we?" she huskily replies.

Grabbing the waistband of my jeans, she begins to pull them and my boxer briefs down. Lifting myself up, I help her get them off. She removes my shoes—throwing them to the side—before pulling my pants and underwear off completely, leaving me in only my dress shirt and socks.

Leaning forward, she begins to undo my shirt buttons. One by one, she pops them open. Once they are all undone, she runs her hands up my abs, sliding her hands across my shoulders, pushing the material down my arms and off.

"It's like you're a god carved from stone," she whispers. Her eyes and fingers tracing the ridges of my torso. "I wanna lick every crevice."

She lifts her gaze to mine and I raise my eyebrows. "Have at it, baby."

"You don't need to tell me twice." Leaning forward, she licks across my collarbone and down my pecs. Her tongue circles my nipple and then she sucks. No one has done this to me before and I have to say, it's an amazing sensation, but what's even more amazing is Kendall's lips wrapped around my cock.

After my nipples, she makes a beeline for my dick. Her tongue darts out, licking the tip before she opens wide and slides my shaft into her warm, wet, waiting mouth.

In and out my cock slides between her pouty lips.

Lifting her hand, she massages my balls. She licks down my shaft and takes a ball into her mouth, sucking deeply before it pops out. She licks back up, circling the tip and pressing her tongue into my slit.

"Suck me," I demand, and being the good girl she is, she obeys my command and sucks me back into her mouth. Her mouth envelops my cock, the tip hitting the back of her throat. Her eyes water but she doesn't stop. Her hand pumps at the base in time to her mouth sucking.

That tingly sensation develops in my balls, and two strokes later, I come down her throat. She drinks every last drop. Pulling herself upright, she wipes at the corner of her mouth. "MMMMMM," she teases, sucking her finger into her mouth. "A Huxley pop is my favourite."

"You dirty dirty minx," I say, shaking my head with a grin worthy of a carnival clown on my face. "What am I going to do with you?"

She stands up and gazes down at me, offering me her hand. "I have an idea...or three."

13

KENDALL

BLOW JOBS AREN'T my most favourite thing to do sexually, but after blowing Hux just now, I think I like them. He wasn't rough. He let me lead, and when he came, holy shit, I nearly did too, and after that epic blowie, I'm ready to combust with desire, want, need, and everything in between. I need him to fuck me, and I need him to fuck me now.

Standing up, I outstretch my hand and make my offer. "I have an idea...or three."

"If your ideas are anything like my ideas, then I'm seven million percent on board." He places his palm in mine and I pull. He stands up and I stare at him. He licks his bottom lip, the silver ball in his tongue twinkles in the light. "I fucking love that tongue ring of yours tracing my body, sliding in my mouth and pussy."

"It fucking loves tracing your body, sliding in your mouth, and being shoved inside your pussy."

Holy fucking shit, this man is going to be the death of

me, but I can unequivocally say, death by fucking Huxley will be a fantabulous way to die.

Huxley laughs.

"What are you laughing at?"

"You know you just said that out loud?"

My eyes widen, "Oh," I reply.

"Oh yeah, but you know what, I agree death by fucking would be a fantabulous way to die, but let's save the dying for another time. My cock needs in your pussy."

"And my pussy needs your cock in it, so let's take this to the bedroom, shall we?" I don't wait for his reply. I turn on my heel and swing my hips side to side as I lead the way to my bedroom.

A loud crack can be heard, and then my ass cheek is burning. Turning around I face Hux. "Did you just slap my ass?" He nods. "Slap it again," I sexily say. Spinning back around, I lean forward and push my ass toward him.

He runs his hand over my cheek, squeezes, and then slaps it...twice. I've never been so turned on. I'm soaked, my arousal drips down my thigh. Clenching my legs, I moan when he hits me again.

"Stop," I pant. "I'm gonna come if you hit me again." And it's true, I'm on the verge of another orgasm.

"Really?" he asks me. Running his hand over my ass, he pushes between my thighs and into my pussy. "Holy shit, you're—"

"Mmmhmpf," I moan as he thrusts his fingers in and out of me. Sliding up my slit, he circles my clit and I come. Closing my eyes, I let the pleasure envelop me and I moan through my release.

Huxley removes his hand, and I miss the feeling of his digits inside of me. Opening my eyes, I look over my shoulder and see him sucking my juices off his fingers.

Turning to face him, I grab his hand and trace his index finger over my bottom lip before slipping it into my mouth and sucking. Removing his finger, I throw my arms around his neck and kiss him.

He wraps his arms around my waist and deepens the kiss. His studded tongue sweeps into my mouth, causing my body to once again come alive. His cock hardens between us, slipping my hand down, I grip his shaft and begin to stroke. He grips my ass and lifts me up, my legs wrap around him, and I grind myself on his dick as he walks toward the hallway.

"Bedroom?" he demands.

"First on the left," I reply, my lips never leaving his.

He enters my bedroom and stops at the end of the bed. One minute I'm in his arms and the next, I'm free falling. Landing on the mattress with a thud and then I'm sliding down the mattress. His hands grip my ankles, and he pulls me down the bed. In one swift action, he drops to his knees and lowers his face to my pussy.

His tongue licks from taint to clit, circling the bundle of nerves and then lowers back down. "Yesssssssss," I mewl. Closing my eyes, I grip my breasts in my palms and massage as he continues to devour me with his tongue. This man is a god with his mouth and fingers, I can only imagine what it's going to be like when he slides his cock deep inside of me.

I'm on the edge of coming again when everything stops.

Opening my eyes, I lift my head and I stare daggers at him, but when I see him standing at the end of my bed, gripping and stroking his cock, all that anger dissipates. "That's so hot," I inform him. Sliding my hand down, I slip my finger between my folds. Tracing the path he took with his tongue only a few moments ago.

With our eyes locked on one another, we pleasure ourselves. It's torture but of the most erotic kind. He must feel it too because he stops and stares down at me. "I need to fuck you now."

Nodding, I stop pleasuring myself. "I need you to fuck me now too."

Shimmying up the bed, I reach into my bedside drawer and remove a foil packet. Rolling to my back, I stare up at him, and beckon him closer with my finger. He kneels on the mattress, and I sit up. I tear open the foil packet with my teeth and sheath his shaft.

Lying back down, I spread my legs wide and wait...I wait for him to slide his dick inside me and send me to paradise.

14

HUXLEY

SHE IS A VISION.

Lying naked on her purple sheets.

Her legs spread wide.

Her arousal glistening in the light.

She's ready and waiting for me.

With my eyes locked on hers, I line my cock up at her entrance and push the head in. Her warmth envelops me, and I know with all the foreplay and earlier orgasms, I'm not going to last long. I just hope I can last long enough for her to come first.

"Please fuck me, Huxley," she pants, and who am I to deny her. With a flick of my hips, I slide balls deep inside of her. We both cry out as I slide in and out. At the ecstasy building, her pussy hugs my cock tight with each thrust.

"Kiss me," she demands.

Lowering my head down, I do as she demands and I kiss her.

Our tongues slide in and out of each other's mouths in sync with my cock slipping in and out of her. I'm close to coming, it's taking everything I have to hold off when she utters two words that are a relief to hear, "I'm coming."

Her body stiffens, her nails scratch down my naked back, and she screams my name, "Huuuuuuuuu-uxleeeeeeey." She crashes over the edge, quivering and mewling as she comes around my cock. Her body squeezes me tighter, and I too come, grunting as I empty my load into the condom.

Collapsing on top of her, I breathe heavily into her shoulder. My chest rapidly rising and falling with each hurried breath I take. "You're squishing me," she squeaks out.

"Shit!" I exclaim. Rolling off her I flop to my back next to her.

Turning my head to face her, she looks to me and I notice her cheeks are stained with that 'orgasmic pink' colour, and I find myself grinning.

"What are you grinning at?" she asks me, rolling to her side.

Rolling to mine, I face her. Lifting my hand, I brush a tendril of hair behind her ear. "You are glowing, and I love the orgasmic shade of pink that's marring your cheeks right now."

"I love glowing like this. Hux, I don't think I've climaxed that hard before."

"Me neither."

Sitting up, I swing my legs over the edge of the bed to remove the condom.

"Oh, shit," she cries out.

At the shrillness of her voice, I stop what I'm doing and look over my shoulder toward her. I see shock all over her face. "What's wrong?"

"Your back," her mouth opens and closes, "it looks like you did five rounds with a lion."

Standing up, I walk over to the mirror in her room and turn to have a look. Sure enough, there are scratch marks all over my back, and I find myself grinning as I take them in.

"Why are you grinning?" she questions. "I've shredded your back."

"I've had worse," I tell her. Her eyes widen and then I realize what I just said. "From the explosion last year. Glass shards and metal fragments were embedded in my back," I explain.

"Oh," she timidly replies.

Removing the condom, I tie it off and drop it in the trash can by her dresser and climb back into bed. Kendall snuggles into my side, and I wrap my arms around her. I've never really been a snuggler, but Kendall being in my arms right now feels right. Our bodies fit together perfectly. Placing a kiss on her forehead, I close my eyes. "That was so worth the wait," I tell her.

"Sooo worth it," she agrees.

"Let me get some shut-eye and we can go again."

"Sounds like a plan."

"A very good plan. Good night, Huxley Weston."

"Good night, Kendall Jones." Placing another kiss on her forehead, we snuggle closer and drift off to sleep, blissfully wrapped in each other's arms.

Fate may have tried to keep us apart but at the same time, she kept having us meet, and this time, this time I will not let anything get in the way of us staying in contact.

15

KENDALL

MY EYES FLICKER OPEN, and a smile graces my face when I see and feel, a muscular arm draped across me, cupping my boob. *Such a boob man.* Turning my head, I see Huxley's mass of dirty blond hair. He's sound asleep on his stomach, so my eyes home in on the scratch marks I left on his back. Reaching over, I trace along the longest one, he squirms under my touch and grumbles incoherently in his sleep.

"Wake up, sleepyhead," I whisper.

"Five more minutes," he whines. Turning his head to face me, he begs. "Please?"

"But I can't do this if you wait." Rolling closer to him, I half cover him with my body and I pepper kisses on his cheek, nose, and finally his lips. He quickly takes control and pushes me to my back, covering my mouth with his for a searing good morning kiss.

"Good morning, Kendall Jones."

"Good morning, Huxley Weston. Did you sleep well?"

"Like the dead. You?"

"Very well."

We stare at one another. "How do you take your coffee?" he asks me.

"Black, one sugar. You?"

"Milk and one. Are you a breakfast person?"

Shaking my head, I scrunch my nose. "Not really, I'm more of a brunch person."

"Breakfast is the most important meal of the day."

"Thanks, Dad," I deadpan. "Seriously, you sleep with a guy and then he thinks he can tell you what to eat?"

"But how will you have the energy to sleep with me again?"

"I can't tell you all my secrets 'cause then I'd have to kill you, and I really don't want to do that because I kinda like you."

"And I kinda like you too." My heart swells at those words. "Since it's past breakfast, how about I take you out for brunch?"

"I'd like that," I honestly tell him. Cupping his cheek in my palm, I stare up at him. "Thank you," I blurt out.

"Thank you for what?"

"For finding me again. I guess the saying, third time's the charm is correct because the first two meetings between us ended shittily, but last night was anything but shit."

"Definitely does not fall into the shit category," he agrees. "I'd place it into the 'freaking amazeballs when can we do it again' category."

Again, I find myself grinning and my heart jumps excitedly at his words. The connection between Huxley and I is strong. We get along well and the sex, holy shit-balls, the sex is freakin' amazing. I'll be surprised if I don't waddle to brunch. A giggle slips out at that thought.

"What's got you giggling?"

"Nothing," I quickly reply, but I know that I answered too quickly.

"Tell me," he urges.

Shaking my head side to side, I try to roll out from under him, but he traps me beneath his body.

"Tell me," he demands. This time he digs his fingers into my side, tickling me. It causes me to flinch and laugh. "Ohhhhhhh, is someone ticklish?"

"No!" I defiantly say but again, I know it's a mistake because from the sinister look on his face, I know he's about to tickle me. Before I even finish that thought, his fingers are dancing across my ribs.

"Stop. Stop," I beg through laughter, which he ignores and keeps tickling me. He lowers his head down and blows a raspberry on my neck, causing me to absolutely lose it. I'm snort-laughing, I cannot remember the last time I laughed this hard. "Stop. Please. I'm gonna pee myself."

That gets him to stop, and it allows me to slide off the bed. Jumping to my feet, I turn and face him. "Gotcha," I tease.

He shakes his head and sits on the edge of the bed. Once again, we stare intently at one another, and within the blink of an eye, he reaches out, grabs my wrist, and pulls me between his legs.

He places a soft kiss on my stomach. Lifting my hands, I run them through the strands of his hair, staring down at him. I can see myself falling for this man. I already have a crush on him, how can I not? He's hot as hell. He has a heart of gold. He's easy to talk to and he seems to love his friends with all his heart.

"Now, who's got who?"

"I didn't realize this was a competition." Pushing him to his back, I straddle his thighs and playfully add, "Now who's got who?"

Before I can even smirk down at him, I'm flying through the air and then I'm on my back. Huxley cocooning me with his body. "Oka—" I don't get to finish because he presses his lips to mine. Wrapping my arms around his shoulders, I kiss him back with everything I have.

Pulling back, he stares down at me. Something passes between us, but before I can question him my stomach loudly rumbles.

"Hungry?"

"Yes," I nod, "but right now, I'm not hungry for food." I'm hungry for this man. He's unleashed something within me, and I'm starved for his cock.

We feed our obsession for each other and after another two mind-blowing orgasms, we come up for air.

"Let's get showered and then I'll take you out for brunch."

"I'd like that." He hops off the bed, and my eyes rake over his naked form. "Shower with me?" I ask him.

"Hell yes, you naked and wet, I'm there."

"Weeelll, I'm currently naked...and I'm pretty sure I'm still wet." Sliding my finger down my chest, I circle my nipple to tease him. I think this teases me more than him, but I'm invested now. Tracing down farther, he reaches out and grips my wrist gently.

"Don't start something that you can't finish."

My movement pauses at the top of my panty line, well it would be if I was wearing any. "Who says I can't finish what I'm about to start?"

"You are a minx."

"You make me a minx," I throw back at him with a wink.

"Well, by all means, continue being a minx."

My heart is racing. Prior to this man, I'd never pleasured myself in front of anyone before, it's called 'self-love' for a reason. I'm nervous to do this in front of him again but when I look up and see his eyes focused on my hand, any hesitation I have dissipates. A wave of courage courses through me and I continue to glide my finger to my slit.

A hiss escapes me when I brush my clit. My finger easily slides down my slit—that'll happen after two orgasms. I look down at myself, something I've never done before and it's oddly erotic watching my finger slide between my folds.

"Push it in," he demands.

Lifting my gaze to his, I watch him watch me as I do what he requested. I press my finger in and out. His cock is rock-hard, I lick my lips when I see the bead of precum glisten in the morning light.

With my other hand, I squeeze my breast, a moan escapes me, and I begin to writhe on my bed. That tingly sensation begins to build low in my belly. With my eyes closed, I focus on tweaking my nipple and pressing my finger inside. Curling it, hitting that magical spot.

"I'm coming," I huskily moan. Groaning through my release, I continue to finger myself through the wave. My body relaxes into the mattress and then I feel a warmth hit me. Opening my eyes, I see Huxley tugging on his cock and thick streams of white hitting my skin and sheets.

"Fuuuuck," he mutters as he continues to milk himself.

He opens his eyes and stares at me. "I'm sorry, I...I didn't mean to."

Lifting to my knees, I shuffle across the mattress to him. My knees hit a wet spot, but I'm not fazed by it at all. Gripping his cheek in my palms, I stare into his eyes. "Don't apologize for one of the hottest scenes I have ever been a part of."

"It definitely was hot and will be locked in the spank bank for future reference. Now, let's get that shower, then I can feed you because after that I'm famished, and I think we need some energy for later."

He throws me a wink and heads into my en suite. My vagina clenches because she hasn't seen this much action in a very, very long time but if I died, I think I'd be okay. I thought kissing Huxley was amazing but getting naked and doing the horizontal tango with him is more than I ever could have imagined.

16

HUXLEY

WELL, this morning has taken a sexy turn that I didn't see coming. When I told her I was locking it in the spank bank, I totally meant that because watching Kendall fingerbang herself was waaaaay better than any porn I've ever watched. And yes, I've watched porn before. A. I'm a man. B. I work on a rig with fifty other guys, a bit of self-love is needed every now and again, and C. I'm a man.

Leaning into the shower stall, I turn the faucets on and wait for the water to heat. The Chainsmokers and Coldplay's "Something Just Like This" begins to play from the other room when Kendall joins me in the bathroom.

Her cheeks are still pink and even with her hair all over the place, she looks fucking stunning. "You really are beautiful, Kendall Jones."

"You, Huxley Weston, need your eyes checked. I look like a mess."

"A hot mess."

"See, mess."

"You missed the hot part. Now get into that shower so I can get you naked and wet."

"I thought we already established that I was naked and wet."

"Wet wet, not aroused wet."

"I thought you liked me aroused wet."

"Oh, I do, but I haven't seen you wet wet yet. Are you going to deprive this poor boy from seeing that?"

"I can't have you upset, so I will oblige and let you see me wet wet and if you play your cards right, you might get to see me naked wet aaaand aroused wet."

"Fuuuuck," I groan. "Get in the shower, woman."

"So bossy," she teases.

The minx saunters past me and runs her fingertip across my chest before she climbs into the shower. "You coming?" she throws over her shoulder before stepping under the spray.

Shaking my head, I laugh at her sass and follow her into the shower. My eyes watch as the water sluices down her body. She reaches out and pulls me under the water stream. My head drops back, and I let the water cascade down my face.

Running my hands through my hair, I open my eyes and step back. This shower is about to get hotter and I'm not talking about the water temperature. Kendall is currently soaping herself up. Her hands are sliding across her skin, her nipples pebbling under her touch. "Fuuu-uck," I groan.

"What's wrong?" she asks, her voice laced with concern.

"Watching you in bed was hot but here, in the shower

with water and steam and bubbles—fuck me sideways—it's…I have no words."

"Is this better?" She pumps more body wash into her palms, turns to face me, and rubs her hands across my chest. The feel of her soapy hands on me heads straight to my cock. I'm now sporting a semi, and she's only soaped up my chest.

"It's not really any better but at the same time, I don't want you to remove your hands."

"Good," she matter-of-factly states and then she drops to her knees.

"Fuuuuck," I groan again. I was expecting her to take me in her mouth, but she soaps up my legs. Her hands getting higher and higher with each rub.

With her eyes on me, she slides her hands around the back of my legs and washes my ass. Squeezing my cheeks in her hand, she winks at me. "Turn around," she demands and like a little lap dog, I spin around to face the wall. She lifts herself up and cleans my back. Her fingertips trace lines up and down my torso.

"Sorry about these," she whispers.

Turning back around to face her, I cup her cheek in my hand. "Don't be. I'm not. I wouldn't change a thing about last night."

"Me neither."

She leans forward and presses her lips to mine. Wrapping my arms around her waist, I kiss her back. Spinning her around, I press her into the tiled wall, and she hisses into our kiss when her bare back hits the cool tiles.

"Huxley," she seductively whispers, "as much as I

would love for you to slide your cock, that's currently pressing into my stomach, into my vagina, she needs a break. But I promise after you feed me, you can slide it in all afternoon long."

"You drive a hard bargain, but I will accept, and even though he's hard right now, I think I'd blow my load in three point five seconds, and you deserve longer than that."

"You say the nicest things to me when your cock is pressing into my stomach, now let's get washed so you can feed me...food."

"Deal." Leaning down, I press my lips to hers for one final searing hot shower kiss.

Pulling apart, we each wash ourselves. Our eyes tracking each other's movements, and if I'm honest, I think this is hotter than if we'd fucked in the shower.

Kendall climbs out first and wraps a bright pink towel around her. She bends down and grabs one from the cupboard for me. She hands it to me and when our fingers brush, a jolt of electricity zaps through us.

She stands in front of the mirror, picks up her tooth-brush, and squeezes some paste onto the bristles, then she pops the brush into her mouth and opens the vanity mirror. She pulls out a spare brush and hands it to me.

"Thanks," I say with a smile. Standing next to her, I too brush my teeth. This feels all domesticated and perfect.

I slip into my clothes from last night, and she pulls on a caramel-coloured sweater dress that hugs her curves and accentuates her tits. Expecting her to take another thirty minutes on her hair and makeup, I'm shocked when less than five minutes later, she joins me in her living room.

Chocolate brown waves cascade down her back and her lips are a shiny peach colour. "You look amazing," I honestly tell her.

"And you look just as good in the daylight as you did last night in those clothes. Did you want to head to your place to change first?"

"Nah, I'm all good. Now let's go, I'm famished."

"Just let me pop my shoes on." She leans behind the sofa and pulls out a pair of black Converse sneakers. This woman shocks me, you'd think with the sexy as fuck dress she'd wear heels, but nope, she complements her dress with a comfy pair of sneakers.

With her shoes on, she links her arm around mine and we exit her apartment. Stepping out onto the sidewalk, I squint at the brightness and really wish I had my sunglasses right now.

"Where to?" I ask her and then together, we say, "Sophie's."

Sophie's is THE best brunch place around, and I always try to eat there at least once when I'm home.

Kendall orders us an Uber and it arrives fairly quickly. Ten minutes later the car drops us off at Sophie's, and as if fate is on our side, we are seated straightaway. Since we both know what we want, we immediately order. She orders eggs Benedict with maple bacon, and I order the breakfast poutine with a side of extra bacon.

"How can you eat poutine at breakfast?"

"Technically it's brunch," I state, and she cheekily sticks her tongue out at me. "But I can eat anything at any time of the day. I guess it comes from doing shift work. When you really think about it, your stomach doesn't know what time of day it is."

"I can see sense to that logic but it's still weird."

"You cannot tell me that you've never had a bowl of cereal for dinner?"

"I can neither confirm nor deny that," she playfully replies, just as our waitress drops off our coffees. "Speaking of cereal, what's your favourite?"

Stirring my sugar into my coffee, I think about it. "You're going to think I am totally boring."

"Let me guess," she taps her chin in thought, "Rice Krispies?" I shake my head. "Corn Flakes?" Again, I shake my head. "Mmhmm." Her eyes widen. "Oh.My.-God, I know, it's Cheerios." I nod. "Please, please for the love of God, tell me that it's at least a flavoured one?" Shaking my head, she stares at me wide-eyed. "Just when you think someone's perfect, they go ruining breakfast with the plainest cereal on the planet."

"What's your choice then?"

"Depends on the day. Some days I'm all for the Lucky Charms. Others it's muesli but then, I also love me some Captain Crunch."

"You are such a big kid. No wonder you and Bryce clicked last night."

"Hello, she was drinking a Shirley Temple, girl's got taste."

A laugh escapes me. "You really are something, Kendall Jones."

"A good something, right?"

"A very good something." We fall silent and stare

across the table at each other. "I'd really like to kiss you right now," I say, breaking the silent stare off between us.

"And I'd really like you to kiss me right now."

Leaning across the table, I brush a tendril of hair behind her ear and place my lips against hers. I was only going in for a quick peck, but when I'm around her all logic disappears, and now, I'm making out with her in the middle of Sophie's. I've never really been a fan of kissing before, but I could quite easily kiss Kendall for the rest of my life.

A clearing throat pulls us apart. Kendall blushes, and I laugh. Sitting back in my chair, the waitress places our meals down and leaves us alone. Quietly we dig into our breakfast and as I eat, I wonder what's in store next for Kendall and me.

17

KENDALL

"OH, MY GOD," I groan. Leaning back in my chair, I rest my palms on my extremely full belly. "I'm sooo full right now. I don't think I'll ever need to eat again."

"I'm sure I can think of a way for us to burn off some of the fullness." He winks at me and I swear, my clit pulsates at what he's insinuating. This man is going to be the death of me...and my vagina. I went from a dry spell between the sheets to a downpour of orgasms, but I'm not complaining. Huxley is an amazing guy, in and out of the bedroom.

Out of the blue, he demands, "Give me your phone." Looking at him quizzically, I stare at him just as the waitress comes and clears our plates away. "Phone, please, Kendall," he asks again.

Digging in my purse, I grab my phone, unlock it, and hand it over. He taps on the screen and I wonder what he's up to. "There, you now have my number, therefore, you can call me anytime."

"I will." I nod and smile, finally it seems like Huxley and I are getting our chance. Third time's a charm and all that shit. My fairy tale happily ever after is finally on track. "I definitely will, Huxley Weston. I definitely will."

We stare at one another, and just like always, the world around me fades into the background and the only thing I see is him. Leaning across the table, he cups my cheek in his palm. He gently runs the pad of his thumb over my lip. We both lean forward and just before his lips press against mine, the waitress reappears. "Can I get you both anything else?"

"Just the bill," we both request at the same time. The two of us laugh at our synchronicity and the waitress rolling her eyes at us.

She returns, and before I have a chance to grab it, he picks it up and walks to the counter to pay. He returns a few moments later. "Ready?" He offers his hand.

Nodding, I place my hand in his and stand up. Lacing our fingers together, we exit Sophie's and begin to walk. Our steps fall into sync, and we chat about our jobs, our families, and everything in between.

Before I know it, it's mid-afternoon and we're almost back at my apartment. I'm pretty sure that we've walked all over the city today.

We stop in the park around the corner from my place and sit on a bench underneath a huge maple tree. "Kendall, I've had an amazing time with you last night and today. I leave for two weeks tomorrow but you have my number, I want you to call and text me while I'm away, and then when I'm back, I want to take you out on an official date."

"I'd like all of that," I honestly tell him. "You'll be so sick of hearing from me while you are away that by the time you get back, you'll be avoiding me."

"I doubt that very much because since I met you on New Year's, you have been at the forefront of my mind."

Those words make me all warm and fuzzy on the inside. I have literally only been with this man for a total of thirtyish hours since New Year's, but I feel like I know him inside and out. We have a connection that's strong, and I cannot wait to explore this connection further.

He leans in and kisses me, closing my eyes. I give everything I have into the kiss. His tongue stud clacks against my teeth, causing me to pull back, breaking the connection. "Ouch," I whisper, rubbing my tooth with my tongue.

"Sorry," he responds, staring at me.

"It's okay, but it was probably a good thing because we're in a park and I was ready to straddle you."

"Fuck, babe, you can't say shit like that to me."

His phone rings and when he pulls it out, his eyes widen. "Shit," he says and then answers. "I know, I know. I'm late. I'll be there in ten."

He hangs up without letting them reply.

"I forgot I was meeting Hayden, Bryce, Ruby, and Danny for drinks and I'm late."

"Oh," I say, sad that our time together is coming to an end.

"Did you want to come with?" he asks.

"Thanks for the offer but I need to do a few things before work tomorrow."

"Oh," he replies, the tone of his oh similar to mine just now. "Let me call you an Uber."

Shaking my head, I cover the phone in his hand with my hand. "I'm just around the block, I can walk."

"Well, let me escort you home."

"I'd like that." We stand up and he laces his fingers with mine. Exiting the park, I lead us back to my place. Sooner than I would have liked, we arrive back at my apartment.

We stop and face one another, and he takes my other hand in his. "I'm going to miss you," he informs me with a grin.

"I'm going to miss you too. How is that possible when we've only been together for twenty-four hours?"

"I have no clue."

We stare intently at one another when a taxi pulls up next to us. A couple climbs out, and Huxley leans down and through the open front window says, "You free?"

The driver nods. "Give me a sec."

He turns back to face me. "Make sure you call me when you get a free moment."

"I will." Wrapping my arms around his neck, I cover his mouth with mine for a searing hot goodbye kiss.

"See you soon, Huxley Weston."

"See you soon, Kendall Jones."

He climbs into the back of the car, and I stand on the sidewalk and watch him drive away. I find myself grinning like the Cheshire cat because this time we said goodbye. We actually said the word and we got in a goodbye kiss.

Walking into the building, my smile increases when I realize I have a way to contact him and that in fourteen days I get to see him again. Huxley and I have something beautiful, and I cannot wait for him to get back.

18

HUXLEY

...Canada Day

RUBY RED LIPS *are wrapped around my shaft. Chocolate brown orbs stare up at me. My cock is rock-hard and watching it slide between her lips is mesmerizing. Her head bobs up and down, faster and faster. I'm ready to blow my load but I need to hold off. The grip on the base of my shaft tightens, the sensation is overwhelming...* A knocking at my door startles me and I open my eyes; it was all a dream.

Well, the part about her on her knees was a dream because my hand is currently wrapped around my rock-hard dick, and I'm on my couch...alone.

"Fuuuuck," I groan, wishing that my dream was a reality.

"Westie, open up, it's me," Hayden yells from the other side of my door.

"Coming," I yell, while internally, I tell myself, *almost.*

There's nothing I can do about my boner right now, so I pull my sweats back up and walk over to the door. Swinging it open, I hide behind it. "You gonna let me in?" Hayden asks, looking confused as to why I didn't just let him enter my apartment.

Seeing that he's alone, I swing it wide and gesture for him to enter.

He steps in and notices my erection, kinda hard to hide it when I'm only wearing sweats. "I interrupt something?" he teases, dropping onto my couch where I was just lying.

"Actually, yes," I inform him as I close the door. "I was sitting right where you are, thin—"

"Ugh, you dirty fucker," he growls, jumping up quickly. "Can't you do that shit in your bedroom?"

"Bonus of living alone, I can jack whenever and wherever I want to jack."

"You really need a girlfriend," he says, shaking his head, taking a seat at my breakfast nook. "Is here safe?"

Nonchalantly I shrug my shoulders. He flips me the bird and all is right between us once again.

"What are you doing here?" I ask, sitting down across from him after grabbing two beers and sliding one across to him.

"Bryce sent me to make sure you don't skip out on today." The last few weeks I've been flaking on hanging with them. I'm just not in a sociable mood at the moment. I'm actually a right grumpy ass after being ghosted by Kendall. I really thought after our weekend together on St. Patrick's Day that it was the start of something beautiful, but I haven't heard from her. I gave her my number so clearly everything I felt was just one-sided.

"It's Canada Day, as if I'd miss this," I tell him and I mean it. "It'd be unCanadian to flake today...plus your wife is scary when she's angry, and pregnant angry Bryce is super Oh-My-God scary." Don't get me wrong, I love his wife but since becoming pregnant, holy crazy hormones. One minute she's happy, the next crying, and then in the blink of an eye, she's hulking out.

"Try living with her...and if you tell her I said that, I'll tell her it was YOU who ate the last of her Tim Tams."

"You wouldn't?"

"Try me," he deadpans.

"Fuck, fine. I'll keep my mouth shut...but I'm sure she's gonna love me when I bring her this." Leaning down beside me, I lift up the hamper I've been putting together: Butterfingers, Bio-Oil, a cute little baby onesie that's a mini boiler suit like what we wear at work. A stuffed beaver. Slippers that I know she's been wanting and a few other luxuries that she wouldn't normally buy herself and Tim Tams. I've included every flavour of Tim Tam on the market right now—the postage getting these here from Australia was ridiculous, but those lil' chocolate-covered biscuits are worth every cent of the postage.

"You're such a suck-up." Hayden shakes his head with a grin.

Shrugging my shoulders, I place the gift back down. "Give me ten and I'll be ready to go."

"You only need ten, I'm disappointed in your stamina, man."

"Fuck you," I spit at my best friend, flipping him off.

Turning my back to him, I walk down the hallway and into my bedroom to get ready for today's celebrations. This year we settled upon a cruise around English Bay. It sets off at 3:00 p.m. and returns six hours later with unlimited drinks and a buffet of never-ending food.

Climbing into the shower, I close my eyes and finish jacking off. Knowing that if I don't, I'll be a pent-up mess all afternoon, and today is not a day to be tense like that.

Feeling refreshed, I pull on my jeans, a red Henley, and my Chucks. I style my hair in that messily styled way and then I join Hayden in the living room...where I notice an empty packet of Tim Tams sitting on my coffee table. "Duuuuuuude, they're for your wife."

"But they're the salted caramel ones."

Shaking my head, I walk to my pantry and pull out another packet to replace the ones Hayd just ate. "Touch these, and the baby Bryce is currently carrying will be the only one you will ever father."

"Why are you so mean to me?"

"Dude, you just ate a WHOLE packet of Tim Tams...by yourself."

"But they're the salted—"

"Caramel ones," I interrupt him, shaking my head. "You never know, maybe your wife will share some with you." He gives me 'the look' and I laugh. "Okay, fair point, but if you behave, maybe I'll share my stash with you."

"I thought you were my best friend."

"I am, but I kinda like your wife more than you...and

wait until the final gift arrives for my hamper, she will totally love me more than you."

He shakes his head and smirks. "Speaking of, we need to go and pick her up so we can get this party started."

"Roger that." I salute him, "let's go." We exit my apartment and make our way over to Bryce and Hayden's place to pick her up.

Late last year, they bought a three-bedroom house in East Vancouver. As soon as I saw it, I knew they'd be starting a family soon, and I was kinda-sorta right since they're pregnant now. It did take longer for them to get pregnant than I thought it would, but what do I know. Regardless of how long it took, this kid is going to be super lucky. Hayden and Bryce are going to be amazing parents and with Uncle Huxley watching over him or her, they'll be a super, super lucky kid.

We pick Bryce up and make our way to Granville Island where the cruise is departing. We meet up with Danny, Ruby, and a few of our other friends. After saying our hellos, with the girls and Danny all cooing over Bryce's expanding belly, we make our way down to the jetty.

Hayden laces his fingers with Bryce's and watching the two of them together makes me smile, but it also leaves me wanting what they have. I thought I might have found my someone, but she ghosted me and now I'm not sure if I'll ever find my other half.

Not wanting to dwell on that, I plaster a smile on my face and follow them up the gangway onto the boat.

We all make a beeline to the bar and once we all have

drinks in hand, we head outside because the sun is shining. It's a fantabolous day weatherwise and will make for smooth sailing.

As soon as I step outside, my eyes widen when I see *her* standing next to a guy, very close to said guy. Her eyes lock with mine, and she seems just as shocked to see me.

Looks like this cruise is going to end like the Titanic, with my heart sinking to the bottom of the ocean.

19

KENDALL

"YOU OKAY, SIS?" Kallen asks me.

Blinking rapidly, I ignore my brother and stare at the man standing across from me. I can't believe he's here. Of all the places to run into him again, it's on a boat. In the middle of English Bay. "Sis, are you okay?" Kallen asks again, squeezing my shoulder. "You're awfully pale all of a sudden."

"Please tell me you see him too," I whisper.

"See who?" he questions. Looking around the boat deck, he shrugs and looks back at me.

"Him."

"Who's him?"

"Huxley." His name quietly passes through my lips.

"Huxley Huxley?"

"Yep." I nod, still staring at him. *Did he get hotter?*

"Huxley who ghosted you Huxley?"

Nodding again, I stare at the man who has plagued my dreams for the last three months, and my memories really didn't do him any justice. He's just as good-looking, if not more so...and then I remember the ghosting and the pain pierces my heart once again.

"Why do you look like you just saw a ghost?" Rarns says, joining Kallen, Chels, and me, handing us our drinks. Taking my drink from her, I chug it back, hoping the alcohol will, well, I don't know what I'm hoping for it to do, but I still feel the same shock so clearly, it did jack shit.

I continue to stare at Huxley, hoping it's a mirage because I'm still not over him ghosting me. She turns her head and follows my line of sight. "That fucking dickwad ghoster," she snarls. "Here." She hands me Chelsea's drink and marches across the deck over to him. I try to hand it to Chels, but she sees I need it and shakes her head. "You have it, babe."

Nodding, I take a sip and watch Rani stalk over to him. Everyone must sense her anger and they step aside, allowing her to pass.

In slow motion, I watch as she stops in front of *him* and throws her cosmo in his face.

That snaps me out of my trance. "Shit," I mumble, and I race over to them, just as she begins her verbal tirade on him. "You dickwad ghoster, you think you can ghost my girl like that and not suffer the consequences? You might be good-looking, but you are a total dickwad ghosterface."

He stares at her, not uttering a word. When Kallen and I arrive, his gaze flits between me and my brother, rage fills his eyes at seeing me which pisses me off more.

Rarns is still laying into him, so glad to have her on my team.

"Remind me never to piss her off," Kallen whispers into my ear and throws his arm over my shoulder. Huxley doesn't like that action and I swear he growls. I can't help but smirk at the jerk face. *Suck it, asshole*, I think to myself as I continue to stare at him.

Rani turns to me and reaches for the drink I'm still holding. I know my bestie and I know she wants to throw another one at him. Shaking my head, I pull my drink out of her reach. "Rarns, don't waste your cocktail like that." I look to him and give him my best death glare. "He's not worth it."

"Come again?" he questions, shocked at my response.

"You're really playing the dumb card right now, asshole?" Kallen spits at him in my honour. I can feel the anger radiating off him.

"Huh?" Huxley utters again. I can feel Kallen getting angrier and I know I need to intervene before my brother does something stupid, something even more stupid than shaving his head and growing a creepy ass mo.

Shaking my head, I pull out from Kallen's arm, turn on my heel to walk away but then I think, *Fuck it*. Spinning back around, I stalk over to Hux and push Kal out of the way. "Just answer me this, why?"

"Why what?" He's genuinely confused right now and that just pisses me off even more.

"Why did you ghost me?"

"Nah, uh. *You* ghosted me. *You* had my number, and *you* didn't call. How was I meant to get in contact with you? I never had your number."

"Is he fucking serious right now?" Kal spits in anger.

"How could I call when I don't have your number," I

snap at him, pissed off that he's putting all of this back on me.

"You do, at brunch, I saved it in your phone."

"Do I look stupid to you? There is no Huxley saved in my phone."

"Give me your phone," he demands, holding out his hand. "I'm going to prove to you that I did give you my number."

"You did NOT save your number, but by all means, have at it." Handing it over, I wait. I know that there is no contact for a Huxley, I've looked through it over and over these last few months.

He taps at the screen and then his pocket begins to ring. He pulls his phone out and sure enough, my number is reflecting back at me on the screen.

"I don't get it," I voice. "I don't have a contact for Huxley in my phone."

"No, you have a contact for Westie." He turns my phone to face me and yep, the name Westie is currently calling him.

"Who the fuck is Westie?"

He lifts his hand and waves at me. "Huxley Weston, also known as Westie, at your service."

My mouth opens and closes in shock. "Are you telling me that I had your number in my phone this whole time?" My voice is laced with shock because I had his digits the whole freakin' time.

"Seems like it." He nods. "At brunch that morning, I saved my number as Westie."

"But I know you as Huxley, or Hux."

"Westie is what most people call me."

"But I don't. Never have."

"For fuck's sake." He shakes his head. He reaches up and cups my cheek in his palm. As soon as he touches me a spark of electricity shoots through me and all the anger at being ghosted evaporates under his touch. My body zings to life in a way that only Huxley can draw from me. "Hi," he quietly whispers. "I'm Huxley 'Westie' Weston or Hux. I've met this amazing girl three times now and fate has been a bitch and interfered, but this time, this time she won't fuck it up. The saying is third time's a charm, but I think the fourth time will be the winner."

"Hi, Huxley 'Westie' Weston or Hux, I'm Kendall Jones and four just so happens to be my new favourite number."

"Mine too," he whispers. Running his thumb along my jawline, I lean into his palm and gaze at him. Even though he's soaked from Rani's drink, he still looks amazing to me.

"Oh.My.God, can these two be any cuter?" Turning my head, I see Bryce and the rest of the people we know all staring at us. Bryce wipes at her eye as if she's crying.

"Aaaand, the waterworks have started, and we've only just pulled away from the dock," Hux teases her.

She sticks her tongue out at him. Her husband pulls her into his side and glares at Huxley. "Back off my wife." He places a loving kiss on her temple and rests his hand on her bump.

My eyes drop and then widen. "Oh.My.God, look at your bump, it's just the cutest."

"I know, right?" Bryce agrees with me, a smile on her face, no longer is she tearing up. "It appeared out of nowhere, and now I feel like I get bigger and bigger each day."

"Tends to happen when you're preggers," my best friend informs us as if we're unaware that that's what happens when pregnant.

"Thank you for keeping us informed, Dr. Rarns."

"You're welcome," she states with a bow. Turning to Bryce, she stretches out her hand. "We haven't officially met, I'm Rani."

Bryce offers her hand. "Bryce." She turns to her husband. "This is my hubby, Hayden," then she points over her shoulder, "and this is Danny and Ruby." She looks to Huxley, and if I didn't know she was happily married, I'd be stabbing her over the look she's staring at Hux. "And you obviously know Westie."

"Now, I know him as Westie." I look over at him and notice his gaze is on me. My grin widens as I focus on him, still not believing he's here. Even though we are on a boat full of people, it's as if everyone around us has disappeared. It's just us and English Bay. "Is this real? Or am I dreaming?" I ask him when suddenly someone pinches my arm. "Ouch," I screech and look over to see that Rarns pinched me. "What was that for?"

"You wanted to know if it was a dream, so I pinched you. FYI, not a dream AAAAAND if you're dreaming about all of us," she circles her finger around the group here, "you are in need of some serious therapy 'cause if I was dreaming about a hot guy, I guarantee it would be just him, me, and lots of nakedness."

"Oh.My.God, I love you," Danny states. "If I batted for your team, you'd totally be mine."

"You couldn't handle all of this, sweetheart, but you can buy me a cocktail since Huxley wore mine and then we can become besties."

"What about me?" I cry out, play pouting at my bestie.

She shrugs her shoulders, links arms with Danny, and the two of them skip, yep literally skip, over to the bar.

"That's gonna be dangerous," Hux says with a laugh. "Better find a life raft now."

A snort-laugh escapes and all eyes turn to me. "What?"

"Did you just snort-laugh?"

"No," I quickly deflect.

"I think you did, Miss Piggy."

"You did not just call me a pig."

"I called you Miss Piggy, there's a difference."

"A pig is a pig."

"But everyone loves Miss Piggy, and have you seen miniature pigs? Fuckin' cute."

"Are you saying you think I'm cute?" I tease.

"Cute. Adorable. Fetching. Sexy. Hot, take your pick."

My cheeks darken at his description of me. "You been reading your thesaurus?"

"Well, I had to do something to pass the time while I was thinking about this cute, adorable, fetching, hot chick."

"You forgot sexy," I tell him on a swallow.

"Sorry, let me try again." He steps into my personal space, sliding his hand around my waist. He leans down and whispers, "Sexy. You are fucking sexy as fuck, Kendall Jones, and I cannot wait to get off this boat."

"Why?" I utter.

"Because I'm going to strip you out of this dress and then I'm going to worship every inch of your delectable body before I sink myself inside of you. You'll be screaming my name for all of Canada to hear."

"Can we get off this boat now?" I breathlessly ask him, just as my brother protests, "Fuck me, Sis, I don't need to hear this shit."

Turning to face him, I glare at my brother. "Kallen, this is Huxley," I offer. "Huxley, this is my baby bro, Kallen." They shake hands, and I can see that my brother is squeezing tighter than is necessary for a 'hello, nice to meet you' handshake. "And his partner, Chelsea." She offers him a shy wave before my dear brother gives him the 'you-hurt-my-sister-I-hurt-you' talk.

"You ever, and I mean ever, intentionally hurt her and I will hurt you. Kendall is my big sis and I will always have her back."

"I will never intentionally hurt her."

"Good," Kallen matter-of-factly states. "I need a beer." And with that, he laces his fingers with Chels, leaving me alone with Huxley.

"Sooo, that's my brother."

"He seems..." Huxley doesn't finish what he thinks of my bro, but I can only imagine it's not pleasant from the look on his face.

"Are you really here? Because fate keeps messing with us and for all I know, this is just a dream. A really vivid amazing dream."

"I'm really here, Kendall." He bites his bottom lip. "I'd like you to come back to my place when the boat docks."

"Can we go now?"

He shakes his head, "Not for another," he looks at his watch, "five hours and thirty-six minutes."

He grips my chin between his thumb and forefinger, leans forward, and presses his lips to mine for a kiss that quickly turns heated. Just like they always do between us. Pulling back, he stares intently at me and my body temperature rises, and it's not from the warm summer's day. It's going to be a loooong five hours and thirty-six minutes.

20

HUXLEY

I WAS LOOKING FORWARD to this cruise to spend some time with my friends, but now that Kendall is here, I'm torn. I want to cruise around with my friends and celebrate but I also want to just hang with Kendall, preferably naked, but since we're on a boat, the naked alone time will have to wait.

That spark between us is just as intense and makes the need to get off this boat so it can be just the two of us that much stronger.

Bryce is an emotional mess right now, so happy that we've met up again, and she made sure to get Kendall's number too so that fate really can't interfere again. I personally think she got her number because she wants to be friends with her, but I saw her first, so she's mine.

Her voice snaps me back to the present, and she utters a phrase that no man ever wants to hear. "Can we talk?"

"That's generally the start to something bad."

She laughs and it's music to my ears. "From my perspective it will be a good talk."

"As long as it's a good one, let's talk."

Crooking my elbow, she slides her hand through, and we head to the bar. I have a feeling liquid courage will be needed. As we walk away, I hear Bryce tearfully say, "Oh, my fucking god, those two are just too cute."

"Pregnant women shouldn't swear," Danny informs her like he always does to poke the beast when she swears at the moment.

And on cue, she sasses, "Fuck you, Danny Boy." And I bet she's sticking her tongue out at him. I glance over my shoulder, and sure enough, she's doing exactly that. I can't help but laugh.

"What's funny?" Kendall questions me as we join the drink line.

"Just the banter between Bryce and Danny."

She nods, and keeps her eyes locked on me. "Is this real? I know I keep asking and Rarns pinched me and all that but..."

Reaching out, I cup her cheek and run the pad of my thumb over her cheekbone. "This is real and I'm really here with you." My lips lift with a smirk. "Should I kiss you so you know it's real?"

She nods and that's all the invitation I need. Stepping closer to her, I slide my hand from her cheek to behind her head and I guide her toward me. Our lips touch and fireworks explode. Doves cry. Angels sing. Cannons fire and confetti rains down from the heavens above.

"I've dreamt about your lips for months now."

"Me too."

Our moment is interrupted when the person behind us clears their throat, looking over, he eyes me and nods toward the bar. The line has moved forward and we haven't.

"Sorry," I quickly apologize and then step forward.

We finally get served, I order her a cosmo and myself a beer. With our drinks in hand, we walk in the opposite direction of our friends, wanting some privacy, but if I know Bryce, she'll be itching to join us.

Leaning on the railing, I look out and notice we're cruising past Stanley Park. I would have thought we'd go the other way so we'd be near the park for the Canada Day fireworks but clearly, I was wrong.

"How have you been?" I ask her, breaking the silence that has fallen between us.

"Good, you?"

"Good."

Well, this is awkward and I don't like it. It's never been like this between us, why is it now?

"Sooo," she says, "this is, ummm…"

"Yep," I reply with a nod and then we fall silent again, but this time there is no awkwardness. Then the silence is broken when we each say the other's name. We both laugh and once again, Kendall snorts.

"I've missed that snort-laugh."

"I call bullshit on that, no one misses a snort-laugh."

"Well, I did."

She nods, "Mmmhmpf," and stares at me, like really stares at me. She reaches up and cups my cheek. "Snorting aside, how did I not know your nickname was Westie or that for the last one hundred and five days I had your number in my phone?"

"You were counting the days?"

"No," she quickly defends. "I'm just guessing."

Pulling my phone out, I ask Siri. "Hey, Siri, how many days since St. Patrick's Day?"

"One hundred and six days since..." she answers.

"Not counting, huh?" I playfully tease, poking her in the ribs.

"I was off by a day."

"Probably because I gave you my number the following day."

"Fine, yes, I may have been counting. I was bummed that you didn't leave your number."

"I stopped by your old place when I got back, that's when I was told you moved."

"Yeah, I was in the process of looking for somewhere new when we met 'cause my landlord didn't want to renew my lease for some reason."

"That sucks."

"At the time yes, but I love my new place, and it's closer to work and Prohibition so it's a win/win." Then she adds on, "But it was a loss that you and I lost contact."

"Not now we won't. I have your number. Bryce has your number."

"Aaaaaand, I have your number saved correctly now." Pulling out her phone, she flashes the screen to me and I see 'HUNKY HUXLEY' saved as my name.

A belly laugh breaks free, pulling my phone out. I tap the screen and update her contact to 'KISSY KENDALL' and then I show her. "We are officially all set on the numbers now." And to reiterate it, I hit dial on her name. Her phone rings in her hand, and when she sees it's me, she begins to laugh.

"Great, it's my stalker again," she complains with an eye roll, followed by a look that has me currently sporting a semi.

"I'm sure I'm the sexiest, I mean hunkiest"—I throw a wink at her—"stalker you will ever have. Now, I think you need to live up to your moniker of Kissy Kendall and kiss me."

"Wow, a guy gets your digits and all of a sudden he's demanding I kiss him."

"Even without your number, I'd demand that. Kissing you is my favourite hobby."

"How is a girl meant to refute that?"

"She's not." I slide my hand around the back of her head and cover her mouth with mine. My tongue slips in and she moans. My semi is now at full mast from that little sound, and my mind is transported back to our night together all those months ago.

Resting my forehead against hers, I stare into her chocolate orbs. "Please come home with me tonight?"

She nods. "There's no place I'd rather be tonight."

As I stare at the goddess before me, I can't wait to have her moaning beneath me. I'm not sure I can wait. My eyes rake over her body and I take in the sexy red and white polka-dot sundress she's wearing. It screams fifties housewife, with a sexy as hell flair, and it looks fucking stunning on her and like usual, on her feet are her favourite, sky-high, matte black stiletto heels—one of these days I'm going to fuck her in just them.

Looking around, I notice that it's just the two of us out here and I'm thankful for that. "I need you, Kendall."

"You have me," she replies.

"No, I need you now."

Her eyes widen as she registers what I'm saying. "I'm not having sex with you out in the open but I'm happy for you to, you know." She wriggles her eyebrows at me.

"To make sure we're on the same page, I'm going to need you to voice what 'you know' is." And I really, really hope she's suggesting that I slip my finger or my tongue between her folds. It's been too long since I've tasted her and my memory needs a refresh. I really can't wait until I can get her back to my place, so I can worship her naked body until I need to go back to work in three days' time.

Running my hand down her arm, her skin breaks out in goosebumps and her cheeks flush with desire.

"I..."

"You what?" I taunt, sliding my hand under the hem of her dress.

"I want you to slide your fingers into me."

"With pleasure," I state. Gently I rub her through the material of her panties, which are soaked. "You're soaked, baby."

"Yes," she mewls, closing her eyes and giving herself over to the pleasure I'm giving her. "Please," she begs, and who am I to deny a sexy wanton woman?

Pushing the material of her panties to the side, I slip a finger into her. Her warmth surrounds my digits, and she moans my name. Clamping her hand over her mouth to not garner the attention of the other partygoers on the boat, I continue to thrust my fingers in and out.

I need to taste her so I drop to my knees and I duck under her dress. I breathe in the scent of her arousal and my already hard cock hardens farther. Leaning forward, I lick from taint to clit, both of us moaning. She tastes better than I remember.

Since we're in public, I increase the thrusts of my fingers and gently nip her clit. This sends her over the edge, and she cries out as she tumbles into orgasmic bliss, coating my face with her release.

Her body trembles stop, and I remove my fingers from her and pull my head out from under her dress. She looks like a goddess from down here. She looks down at me and her eyes widen. "Holy shit, your chin is soaked."

"I'm not complaining and neither were you a few moments ago."

She slaps my arm. "Fiend."

"Only for you, baby, only for you," I reply as I stand up and face her. She grips the lapels of my shirt and pulls me to her. She kisses me deeply, moaning into my mouth.

"I kinda like the taste of me on you."

"I fucking love it," I eagerly reply, "and you know what I love better?"

"What's that?"

"That you love the taste of you on me."

Her cheeks darken in...embarrassment? Arousal? A bit of both? Whatever the reason, she's fucking gorgeous and I'm not letting her go. Fate won't interfere this time.

We continue to stare at one another and then we hear a bang, the Canada Day fireworks are going off all around English Bay. We've been sitting here talking, and other things, for near on three hours now. I'm surprised our friends, specifically Bryce, haven't come and demand that we rejoin them.

We both look to the sky. I watch the fireworks for a few moments and then I focus on the goddess beside me. Reaching out, I pull her to me. Her back to my front. She rests her arms on mine and together we watch the light show and I have to say; I think this is my most favourite Canada Day in the history of Canada Days.

After the firework show finishes, we head inside and join our friends. The rest of the cruise passes by in a blur and before I know it, the boat is docking, and the cruise has come to an end. That was the longest six hours in history, but I'm glad that it was spent with Kendall, getting to know her on a deeper level. Plus it was a bonus that she got to know my friends too. We discovered that Bryce knew Kendall's grandfather. Her grandad was the man who used to order flowers from Bryce for his wife each week. Such a small world.

Don't get me wrong, it has been great being with everyone, but now, now I'm ready to get reacquainted with Kendall and her body.

"You two are too cute to boot," an inebriated Rani rhymingly slurs as we disembark the boat. "I'm so happy you finally get your happily ever after."

"Me too, Rarns, me too," Kendall replies and pulls away from me, linking arms with her friend. She looks over to me and winks and, fuck me sideways, that one little action has my cock twitching.

Our group walks along the gangway and as soon as we hit dry land, we stand around and discuss what we will do now. Bryce and Danny are discussing options, I don't care what we do. As long as I'm with Kendall, I'll be happy. But deep down, I want to get her home and naked.

Wrapping my arms around her like I did while we watched the fireworks, I breathe her in. I close my eyes and savour the moment.

"Did you just smell me?" Looking over her shoulder, she stares up at me questioningly. Her brown eyes glow in the moonlight, shimmering like the chocolate river in *Charlie and the Chocolate Factory*.

"Yep," I unabashedly reply. "I was starting to forget what you smelled like."

"That's kinda creepy...but also sweet."

"What can I say, I'm creepily sweet."

She spins around, drapes her arms over my shoulders, and presses her lips to mine. Over the last few hours, we have kissed...lots...but this one is by far my favourite because she instigated it.

"Spend the night with me?" I ask her.

"I already said I would, but is it for only one night?"

Forever, is at the tip of my tongue but my brain kicks into gear and takes over. "For starters."

"I'll take that," she replies, suddenly shy, but her answer is all I needed to hear. Grabbing Kendall's hand, I yell out a goodbye over my shoulder to our friends and drag her to the taxi lineup. We wait in line and a few moments later, a taxi pulls up. Opening the back door, I usher her in and slap her delectable ass. She squeals and looks over her shoulder at me. Winking, I climb in behind her and give the driver my address.

I cannot wait to get her back to my place.

21

KENDALL

SITTING NEXT to Huxley in the taxi, my heart starts to nervously race, but at the same time, a calmness and feeling of contentment wash over me.

"What are you thinking, Kendall Jones?"

Looking over at him, the streetlight illuminates his face and as I stare at him, the nerves dissipate, and my heart rate returns to normal. "A few moments ago, I was nervous, my heart erratically racing but looking at you just now, the nerves disappeared."

"And how do you feel now?"

My cheeks heat when I realize I'm aroused.

"Going by the shade of pink on your cheeks right now, I think I know how you're feeling." He leans over to me and whispers, "And I bet if I slide my hand under your dress right now, I'll find your panties soaked."

Pressing my thighs together, I realize he's right.

"Bingo," he states, nipping on my earlobe. "I can't wait to get you inside and..."

"And what?" I breathlessly ask.

"Wouldn't you like to know?" he taunts me. Bopping the tip of my nose, he pulls back and looks out the car window.

"You're an ass," I tell him.

"You love my ass."

"That's debatable right now." I huff, crossing my arms. I notice his gaze drops to my breasts and since he taunted me, it's my turn to return the taunt.

Pushing my arms together, my cleavage increases. Glancing at the driver, I notice he's focused on the road—thankfully. Sliding my thumb up, I circle my nipple through the material of my dress. Feeling daring, I pull the material down and slip my thumb and forefinger in. Gently I tug and squeeze my nipple. Biting my bottom lip, I hold back my moan. My eyes are locked on Huxley. His are locked on my chest and full of hunger. He must sense me looking at him because he lifts his gaze to mine.

We stare at one another as I continue to fondle my breast. Our eyes fused to one another, his occasionally dropping to my boobs. He licks his lips and it's the hottest thing ever, seeing his tongue stud sparkle in the street-lights. I want those lips wrapped around the nipple I'm playing with. I just want him to touch me, I'm ready to combust here.

As if he's in my mind, he lifts his hand and covers mine. His dwarfs mine and he easily takes control. He massages my breast while I continue to tweak my taut peak. Biting my lip again, I swallow down my moan, but a tiny squeak slips through my lips.

Huxley leans over and presses featherlight kisses to my neck. My head drops back, the combination of his lips on my skin, his hand massaging my breast, and me tweaking my nipple, it's almost too much but at the same time not enough. I wish we were naked in his bed.

"I wish that too," he whispers.

My head lifts and my eyes are wide open in shock; I can't believe I said that out loud. My reaction causes Hux to laugh. Pushing his hand away, I move mine from my dress and scowl at him. "It's not funny," I whisper-snarl. "What if the driver heard?"

"I'm sure he's heard worse."

Crossing my arms again, I pout. "Don't pout, babe."

"I'll pout if I want to pout."

"Well, lucky for you, we've arrived at my place, and as soon as the door to my apartment closes, it won't be opening again until I have to leave for the airport, and that means everything you want me to do to you is going to happen...twice."

"Promises, promises," I taunt. I hand some cash to the driver to pay the fare and then I climb out. Huxley follows and takes my hand in his. We enter the building and wait for the elevator, the air around us thickening by the second. My heart is once again racing, I cannot wait for what's about to happen.

22

HUXLEY

THE ELEVATOR IS TAKING FOREVER to arrive, well it feels like forever. My cock is painfully pressing against my zipper and with each passing second, that pain and my hardness increases.

When Kendall started to fondle herself in the taxi, I thought I was going to bust a nut. She's sexy and vivacious at the best of times, but tonight, she's all that and more.

Finally, the elevator doors open, gripping her hand, I drag her into the metal car and press the button for my floor. Before the doors have closed, I have her pressed against the back wall and I'm kissing her. Our tongues dance. Our teeth collide. The kiss is frenzied and filled with want. Need. Desire and everything in between. My palm cups her boob, gently massaging. I can't wait to get her into my apartment, and I can do this with nothing between us.

Someone clears their throat and looking over my

shoulder, I realize that we're in the basement. Seems we went up to my floor and back down again.

Kendall lowers her head in embarrassment as my neighbour steps into the elevator with us. I head nod at him and press the button for my floor, again. The doors close and we make our way up. The car is silent as we ascend to my floor, Kendall snuggles into my side, she hasn't lifted her head since he stepped in. We reach my floor, and the doors open, I take her hand in mine, and we step out into the bright hallway.

Just as the doors are closing, my neighbour winks at me and yells out, "Have a good night."

Nodding my head, I can't contain my smile or the chuckle that escapes me when Kendall leans into my shoulder and whispers, "Oh, god, that was so embarrassing."

"At least we weren't fucking," I nonchalantly tell her with a shrug.

Her eyes widen in shock as she shakes her head at me. "With an attitude like that, we won't be."

"I call bullshit, Kendall Jones." I raise my eyebrows at her. "I bet right now your pussy is throbbing. Your panties are drenched and your heart is racing in excitement." She swallows deeply as she processes my words. "And going by that swallow, I'm correct."

"Am not," she snaps, "Now open the door, I need—"

"To fuck, better be the next two words out of your mouth."

"I was going to say use the bathroom, but if you're into golden showers, then I'm sure I can oblige. Personally, I'd rather use the toilet and then ride you all night long."

"You had me at ride you," I inform her.

Grabbing her hand, I drag her down the hallway to my apartment. I unlock and open the door faster than I ever have before. Kicking it shut behind her, I pull her through the living room, down the hall, and into my bedroom. "Bathroom's there." I point to my en suite and gently push her toward the entrance.

"Eager much?" she asks over her shoulder as she steps in.

"Very much so, Kendall Jones, now hurry up and pee."

She shakes her head and closes the door. I stand here and watch the door, impatiently waiting for it to open, and when it does—fuck me sideways—I'm given the view of the sexiest thing I've ever seen.

Kendall is standing there in nothing but a barely-there G-string, with her hip cocked to the side, her high heels, and her hands are cupping her bare breasts. The hidden breasts add to the sexiness of her right now.

"You are a vision, Kendall Jones," I honestly tell her. My eyes rake over her from head to toe once again, searing this vision into my memory for future spank bank referencing.

"What's with the full name references this evening?"

"I don't know," I nonchalantly reply, "I just like saying your name."

"Kendall is just fine."

"Okay, Kissy Kendall."

"Oh God—"

"That's what you'll be screaming soon."

"Cocky much?"

"Very." I grip my junk and wiggle my eyebrows at her.

"You have too many clothes on."

"I can fix that." Quicker than ever, I kick off my shoes, pull my jeans down, and remove my shirt. Leaving me in my underwear, just like her.

"Much better," she states. She covers both her breasts with her arm and beckons me forward with her finger.

Standing my ground, I shake my head and lift my finger, beckoning her to me.

She shakes her head back. We silently stare at one another, neither one of us making a move. The air around us thick—much like my cock—with arousal.

"Just give in, babe."

"Why don't you?" she sasses back.

Before she has a moment to process what I'm doing, I step toward her, wrap my arms around her hips, lift her up, and throw her to the mattress. She squeals with a laugh and the sound has my already hard cock hardening further.

Climbing onto the bed, I cover her body with mine and stare down at her. "I win," I inform her. Lowering my head, I take her nipple into my mouth and suck deeply. Circling the tip with my tongue stud, I gently nip the taut peak, garnering a guttural groan from Kendall.

"I think I win," she breathlessly pants. Running her fingers through my hair, she holds me to her chest and I don't mind at all.

Kissing along the valley of her breasts, I repeat the process on her other nipple. "More," she pants.

Lifting my hand, I massage the breast I was just sucking.

"Yesssss," she mewls.

"More."

"Fuuuuck," she screams, "I'm coming."

Her body stiffens beneath me and she begins to convulse as her orgasm ripples through her.

When her body relaxes, I lift my head and stare up at her, amazed that she came just from that.

"Holy shit, I've never done that before."

"Me neither," I agree, and it's the truth. I've never been with a girl who came from breast play before.

"I think it's that metal ball, that just takes everything to the next level."

"We should test that theory."

"How so?" she asks, reaching up to cup my cheek.

Pressing a kiss to her palm, I tell her my thoughts. "Well, you came from me just sucking your boobs, let's continue the experiment and see if I can make you come all over my face with me only using my tongue."

"Well, in the name of science, I think we should try."

She widens her legs. "Class is in session," she says with a wink.

Kissing down her stomach, my tongue circles her belly button. I flatten my tongue and lick over her belly and down to her panty line. "I hope you're not overly attached to these."

"Huh?" she voices just as I tear her barely-there panties from her body, the material disintegrating with the force of my pull. Her eyes widen when she realizes what I've done but when she feels the first flick of my tongue over her sensitive bud, her eyes widen farther and she moans. Spreading her legs wider, I slide down farther and situate myself between her thighs.

"You have such a pretty pussy." I lick down her slit and push my tongue inside. "And you taste like heaven."

"Less talking, more tonguing." She grips the side of my head and presses me into her mound.

Not needing any further encouragement, I lick and suck her until she is writhing beneath me and screaming my name.

"Science wins, that piercing is the best invention ever."

"I think my cock can do a better job."

"Well, in the name of science, let's see."

Reaching into my side table, I grab a condom, tear it open, and quickly roll it down my shaft. Lining myself up at her entrance, I gently push inside. Her pussy hugs my cock tightly as I slide in and out. Lowering myself down, I kiss her deeply. My tongue sliding into her mouth in sync with my cock.

"I'm close," she pants into my mouth.

Increasing my thrusts, it's what she needs and she screams as orgasm number three unleashes. Her guttural moans set me off, and I empty my load into the condom.

Pulling out of her, I remove the condom and throw it into the trash. Lying down beside her, she snuggles into me. "I think sex science is my new favourite subject and my teacher, Hunky Huxley, is so fucking hot and magical with his tongue."

"Hunky Huxley is happy to oblige. Now rest up because I think we need a refresher before the upcoming exam."

"Who knew studying could be so much fun?" She presses a kiss to my chest. "Good night, Hunky Huxley."

"Good night, Kissy Kendall Jones."

Placing a kiss on her forehead, we both drift off to sleep, blissfully happy and content.

23

KENDALL

THAT WAS the best Canada Day I have ever had, and it's all because of the man sleeping beside me. Rolling to my side, I stare at him, not quite believing that I'm in his bed. After all the previous mishaps, I expected this to all be a dream but it's not. It's my reality and now that I've found him, again, I'm never letting him go.

I was a goner after that first kiss, one kiss just wasn't enough with this man.

Reaching out, I run my fingertip down his cheek. His lips lift into a small smile, he opens his eyes, and his green orbs are vibrant in the morning light.

"Good morning, Kissy Kendall Jones."

"Really, we're starting with that again?"

"Okay, how about, good morning, gorgeous?"

"Much better." Leaning over to him, I place a kiss on his lips. "Good morning, Hux."

"I love it when you call me Hux."

"I love calling you Hux."

We lie here staring at one another when his phone rings. He makes no move to answer it. No sooner does it stop ringing, it starts again.

"Do you need to get that?"

"Nope," he matter-of-factly states. "I'm exactly where I need to be."

That sentence warms my heart. Reaching up, I cup his cheek when my phone begis to ring. It's muffled and then I realize it's still in the living room where I dropped my purse last night.

"Do you need to get that?" he huskily says, the deep timbre of his voice vibrates through me.

"Nope, I'm exactly where I need to be."

He smiles at my reply and it lights his face, and my heart, up. Then BOTH our phones begin to ring. "I think we need to answer."

"I think so too." I nod in agreement.

Climbing off the bed, I walk out naked to my purse. Grabbing my phone, I see it's Bryce but it stops ringing before I get to answer. Padding back to the bedroom, I notice Hux has his phone in his hand. He looks up. "Bryce?"

Before I have a chance to reply, my phone rings again. Jumping back into bed beside Huxley, I answer, "Good morning, Bryce."

"Morning? It's afternoon, you hussy, and you guys are late for drinks."

"Drinks?" I question, scrunching my face up in confusion.

"Every time the guys go away, we do drinks and dinner together You guys are officially late. Now put some clothes on and come join us. Westie knows where."

Before I can reply, she hangs up. "Seems we, well you, are late for your night before leaving catch-up." Looking over to him, I shrug.

"Ahh shit, I don't wanna leave this bed but…"

"Well, let me get out of your hair and you can get going."

"No," he shouts. "I want you to come."

"I can't intrude on your tradition."

"You can and you will."

"If you insist."

"I most definitely insist and if you're a good girl, I'm sure my tongue will show you some attention when we get home."

"You drive a hard bargain and I'd love to…but can we stop at my place so I don't have to wear last night's dress?"

"But I love last night's dress."

"And I bet you'll love today's outfit too."

"Fine," he relents.

We climb into the shower and two orgasms later, we jump into his car and head to my place. I race upstairs and change, earning myself a wolf whistle when I re-emerge fifteen minutes later.

I'm in a black halter top tucked into a flowy boho skirt, and I'm wearing black wedges, giving my heels an afternoon off.

"How do you look that good in just fifteen minutes?"

Shrugging, I slide into the seat next to him. "So, where too?"

"Nightingale's. It's been a tradition since Bryce and Hayden got together that we catch up there before we go back to work."

"It still blows my mind that she's the florist Pops always said was an angel."

"It really is a small world," he agrees, pulling out into traffic and driving to meet up with Bryce and Hayden.

We park the car in a nearby lot, and as we're walking down the sidewalk to Nightingale's, he laces his fingers with mine. I look down at our joined hands and find myself grinning. I'm not usually the hand-holding type of girl, but with Huxley, I find I love all the little touches.

"You two are just too cute," Bryce singsongs as we join them. She jumps up and wraps her arms around me, hugging me tightly. For a wee lil' thing, she sure is strong.

"Sorry, we're late," I tell her, "I wasn't aware there was a tradition, had I known, I would have set an alarm. I hate being late so I really am sorry to have kept you waiting." When I finally take a breath, all three of them are staring at me. "Sorry, I waffle when I'm nervous."

"Nothing to be nervous about," Hayden says, "we don't bite."

Bryce's cheeks darken at his comment, and I'm pretty sure she's thinking dirty thoughts right now. When I look over to Hux, I can tell that his thoughts are also in dirty town.

"Behave," I whisper, taking the seat he's holding out for me.

"Where's the fun in that?" He winks and takes the seat next to me.

We all pick up our menus and start looking at them.

Huxley shimmies his seat closer to me and then I feel his hand on my thigh. Covering his hand with mine, I smile at him. And then my eyes widen when he slides our joined hands between my thighs and up toward my lady parts.

Looking across the table, I notice that our companions are engrossed in their menus. I'm thankful for that because Huxley is currently rubbing my clit with my finger through my skirt.

"Behave," I repeat through clenched teeth.

He winks and then starts a conversation with Hayden about the new project they're starting on tomorrow. I'm close to coming when the bastard removes his hand and picks up his water glass, taking a sip. He winks at me, leaving me high and dry.

Pursing my lips, I stare daggers at him and then decide that two can play at this game. I slide my hand over and grip his junk, not hiding the fact that I'm doing this from his friends. Squeezing tightly, he chokes on his water. "I win," I defiantly tell him.

Removing my hand, I pick up my menu and ask, "So, what's good here?"

"Oh, I love you," Bryce says, grinning ear to ear. "I've never seen anyone leave Westie speechless before." She focuses on him. "Don't let this one go."

"Not planning to, Bryce. Not planning to now that I've found her again."

His comment to Bryce warms my heart. I'm falling for this man, hard. How can I have such strong feelings for someone I hardly know? Sure, we connect in the bedroom, we connect very well behind closed doors, but we also connect outside too. Our friends all get along, which is a bonus 'cause there's nothing worse than being in a relationship and not getting along with the friends.

The afternoon flies by and before I know it, we are back at Huxley's place on the sofa watching Netflix. A laugh escapes me.

"What's so funny?"

"Right now, we're Netflix and chilling."

"Aaaand that's funny because?"

"Netflix and chill," I state.

"Aaaand."

"Really, you don't know what I'm getting at?"

"Nope." He shakes his head and looks really confused right now.

"According to *Urban Dictionary*, Netflix and chill is slang for going over to someone's house and getting down and dirty while Netflix is playing in the background."

"So what you're saying right now is that you want to have sex with me while Netflix is on in the background?"

"Not what I'm saying." Shaking my head, I wave my hands around. "Never mind. Forget I said anything."

"No, no, no, you can't do that. I genuinely want to know why you brought it up."

"It's just we are literally watching Netflix and chilling, but that's not what it means. I just thought it was funny."

"So you don't want to have sex with me?"

"I never said that, I just said we are watching Netflix and chilling."

"I'm so confused right now...and all I can think about

is you riding my dick right here," he pats the sofa next to him, "while we watch Netflix."

"I'm sure I can make that fantasy a reality."

And I do...several times before Huxley carries me into the bedroom where we fall asleep wrapped in each other's arms.

24

HUXLEY

WAKING THE NEXT MORNING, I feel both happy and sad. Happy to be heading back to work with Hayden because we're starting on a new project with Troy up in Kitimat and it's reignited my love for this job but I'm sad, because I'm leaving Kendall behind and we've only just refound one another. I'm shit scared that fate is going to fuck this up for us; again.

"Why are you thinking so loud?" Kendall sleepily whispers from beside me. "It's too early to be thinking like that." Rolling half on top of me, she stares down at me and even with bed messed hair and sleep in her eyes, she's still the most beautiful woman I have ever laid my eyes upon. "What's on your mind, Hunky Huxley?"

"You," I honestly tell her. "I'm excited to be going back to work and starting this new gig, but I don't want to leave you. The last few times that's occurred, we've lost each other."

"But this time will be different."

"How do you know?"

"I just do. Fate had to test us to make sure we were solid, and I think we've proven to her that the pull between us is strong. Nothing and no one can keep us apart."

Leaning down, she gently presses her lips to mine. The kiss starts off soft but as with us, it quickly turns heated. My morning wood hardens between us and an overwhelming need to be inside her builds. Flipping her to her back, I cocoon her underneath me and continue to assault her mouth with mine. She spreads her legs and I slide between them. My cock slips easily inside her and gently we rock our hips, back and forth.

We've been together before, but this time it feels different. It's more than just a fuck, it's like we're making love. My heart stutters at that thought but rather than fear taking hold, contentment washes over me and I continue to make love to the woman who has become my everything.

Together, we tumble over the edge. Our lips never part as we ride out the pleasure coursing through our bodies. Once it passes, I lift up and stare down at her. This moment is perfect and will be seared in my brain forever.

Kendall offers to drive me to the airport, and I happily agree, I want to spend as much time as possible with her. Once we arrive at the airport, I think she'll just drop me off, but she surprises me and enters short-term parking.

Parking the car, we exit. I grab my bag from the back and join Kendall on the pathway. Lacing my fingers with hers, we quietly walk toward the terminal. Once inside, I check in and with my boarding pass in hand, I head back to where she's waiting for me.

We walk over to the coffee shop and grab two coffees. Pulling my phone out, I send a text to Hayden to see where he is.

WESTIE: *Already checked in, where you at?*

Before I've put my phone down, it pings.

HAYDEN: *Not flying out 'til tomorrow, Bryce had cramps and we're at the hospital.*
WESTIE: *Shit, is everything okay?*
HAYDEN: *Just waiting on the OB. Emergency isn't concerned but Bryce is a mess*
WESTIE: *Maybe you should skip this swing???*
HAYDEN: *Thinking about it*
WESTIE: *Don't think, do it. Look after your wife and my nephew*
HAYDEN: *Look at you being all daddy protective. You'll make a fine dad one day, Huxley Weston*
WESTIE: *I've only just gotten the girl. I'm not you, I don't marry someone after seven days*
HAYDEN: *No, it takes you seven months to find her again*
WESTIE: ***middle finger emoji***
WESTIE: *Just look after your girl and my nephew… keep me posted*
HAYDEN: *Will do…thanks, man*

"Everything okay?" Kendall asks.

"Bryce is in the hospital, Hayden isn't coming."

"Is she okay?"

"Not sure exactly. They're waiting on the OB but the ER peeps think everything is okay."

"I bet she's freaking out."

"Yep, hence why Hayden is giving this swing a miss."

"Will your boss be okay with that?"

"Yeah, Troy's cool. A hard-ass at times but he's fair, especially when it comes to family."

"That's good to hear." She takes a sip of her coffee and looks over to me. I'm considering asking her to check in on them for me while I'm away, but I can't ask her to do that, can I? And as if she's a mind reader, she asks, "Would you like me to check on Bryce tomorrow for you?"

"I was just wondering if I can ask you to do that for me."

"I'd be happy to. I really like Bryce."

"Everyone loves Bryce." Reaching across the table, I cover her hand with mine. "Thank you, I really appreciate it."

"I'd do anything for you, Huxley."

"Anything?" I wriggle my eyebrows at her.

"Not that," she informs me.

"Just so I know, what 'that' are we referring to?"

"Butt stuff. That's a one-way passage and it ain't going in."

"Duly noted, and for the record, I'm not down for that either."

"Duly noted but I can say, that has never crossed my mind to do to you. How would I even do that to you?"

"Toys. Cucumbers. Fingers."

"Wow, you've really thought about this."

"No, I've watched a lot of porn offshore."

"Sure, blame the porn."

We both burst out laughing, this is one of the things I love about being with Kendall. We can laugh and talk about anything without it being awkward and weird. The overhead speaker crackles and my flight is called. I deflate at the thought of leaving. "That's my flight," I sadly inform her.

"Oh." She seems just as sad as I am that the time for me to go has finally come.

We stand up and start walking toward security. She stops and stares at me. Reaching up, I brush a tendril of hair behind her ear. "I'll call you when I land."

She nods. "I'd like that. I'd like that very muchly."

"Good. Until then, Kissy Kendall."

"Kissy Kendall, really? In public? Being saved in your phone as that is enough, we don't need to verbalize it when others can hear."

"Whatevs," I tell her. "But there's method and logic to your nickname."

"Oh yeah, how so?"

"You see..." I slide my arm around her waist and pull her to me. "I love kissing you, and I will be thinking about your luscious lips until I get to kiss them again."

Resting my forehead against hers, I close my eyes and breathe her in. Everything around us fades away and all I see is her. This time when we part it won't be as horrendous because finally, I have her digits and for the first time ever, I'm getting a proper goodbye at the airport. "I need to go now."

"I know." She nods. "I'll walk you to security." She pulls away from me and laces our fingers together. We reach security and I tug on her hand, halting her. She turns to face me, and I lift my hand, cupping her cheek. "You really are beautiful, Kendall. I was starting to think fate hated the thought of us as an us with all our encounters and misfortunes."

"Seems four really is our lucky number."

"So, I should kiss you seven times then?"

"How do you get seven from four?"

"Well, once wasn't enough. Four was our luck changing and seven, well it's my favourite number and you've become a favourite of mine, so I'm combining my two favourites."

"Fair enough, but I'm not placing a number on it because you can kiss me forever, Hunky Huxley."

"Can't really argue with that logic, and FYI, I will happily kiss you forever, Kissy Kendall Jones."

She smiles at me and leans in for the first of our seven kisses.

We share one final not-really-suitable-for-an airport kiss and then I walk through security, happy and content for the first time in a long time. Life is finally perfect and I cannot wait for the future.

25

HUXLEY

...ten days later

WELL, this trip has been an epic shitshow. First my flight was delayed five hours due to a mechanical issue just before take-off. That's five extra hours I could have spent with Kendall. Then the shuttle from the airport to Kitimat broke down in the middle of nowhere and then finally, when Troy and I arrived in Kitimat, the hotel couldn't find our reservation. Eventually we got a room, but for the first seven nights I had to bunk with Troy. My boss is awesome, but fuck me sideways, is he an animal. He managed to destroy the room—his clothes were strewn everywhere, the mess he'd leave in the bathroom was mind-boggling and his bathroom habits are disgusting. No wonder he's forty-seven and single, no woman would ever put up with that shit.

Thankfully, I finally have my own room now...only took seven nights of sharing with Piggy McPiggerson also known as Troy, my boss.

My only sanity has been my texting with Kendall. Not being able to get any privacy, we haven't been able to FaceTime, but in the last three days of having my own room, we've made up for that.

I've just gotten off the phone with Hayden, Bryce was released the day after I left, but she needs to take it easy. Ha, I'd pay to see that. That woman doesn't know how to relax so this should be interesting to see, but I'm ever so glad that she and the baby are okay. I don't envy Hayden right now, I'm sure he'd rather be here dealing with this mess instead of his bedridden pregnant wife.

Finishing up lunch, I head back out with the guys. We're here overhauling the valves on rig two and it's my job to make sure everything runs smoothly. The team I'm overseeing all seem to know what they're doing but for each valve we fix, it feels like we discover four other issues.

The next valve on the schedule should be an easy one as there's nothing in the way access-wise. Fingers crossed it will be a simple remove and replace. Right now, we're just waiting for operations to isolate the valve and then we're good to go.

Once given the all-clear, Troy, Kenneth, two lackeys and I head into the plant. The five of us work together in sync and removing the valve goes seamlessly. "Maybe our luck with the job is changing," Kenneth, the new guy, states as we begin to attach the rigging to the new valve ready for the crane to install it.

Troy and I look at one another, our eyes wide. Everyone knows you never voice that out loud because it always jinxes things, but it seems Lady Luck is finally on our side because this one goes back in smoothly, no issues at all.

"Seven down, forty-one to go," Kenneth chortles as we start removing the bolts holding the next valve in place. This is his first stint and his eagerness reminds me so much of me back when I first started.

"Hey, Troy," I yell out, "remember when we first started doing this job and we were as gung-ho and positive like wee Kenneth here?"

"There's nothing wee about me," he refutes, letting go of the tag line he's holding, he cups his junk and thrusts his hips back and forth.

Turning my head toward him, I watch in slow motion as he tries to catch the tag line he just let go of to cup his junk. The valve we'd just removed begins to drop. I'm standing in the wrong spot and the valve swings toward me, colliding with my head and sending me flying backward. I hit the wall behind me with a thud and fall to the grid mesh floor.

The valve lands on my left arm, crushing it and trapping me. I cry out in pain. People are yelling. Feet are thundering on the mesh, racing around to try and free me. The noise echoing around me is deafening. The last thing I see before darkness engulfs me is the valve on top of my arm.

Everything is muffled.

Everything hurts.

I've never felt fuzzy like this before and I don't like it.

There's pressure on my left side, my head is throbbing, and my body feels like it's floating. I'm trying to open my eyes but I can't, it's like there's a lead weight holding them shut.

"Call an ambulance," someone shouts. Ambulance? *Why do we need an ambulance to change a valve? Nothing is making sense right now.*

"Huxley, dude, can you hear me? Open your eyes for me, eh." The voice is muffled and vaguely familiar.

"I can hear you," I say, but my voice echoes and it doesn't sound like me. Like it's me but not.

"Huxley, buddy, open your eyes," they repeat.

I try to do as they ask but nothing. That floating feeling intensifies, I feel weightless and numb, except for the weight pressing down on my left arm.

The pain is turning into a tingling feeling. My body temperature is rising, but at the same time, I feel cold.

"Huxley, buddy..." they say again, but the end of the sentence fades away.

"I can hear you," I shout, but once again, it echoes inside my head. *Why can't they hear me?*

Just as I think this, a searing pain shoots through my arm, up my neck, and into my head. It's excruciating, I've never felt pain like this before. My whole body feels like it's being pressed in a vise; I scream out in agony. My heart begins to race, something isn't right. Everything in my head is echoing and no matter how much I screech in pain or shout, no one hears me. I'm trapped in my mind, and I realize I'm the only one who can hear me right now.

Wind is rushing past me; people are talking but I don't understand anything they're saying. It's like I'm underwater, weightless but sinking. Everything begins to fade again and my last thought is, what the fuck is going on?

26

KENDALL

TEXTING with Hux has been the highlight of my day since he left. Getting home and FaceTiming the last two days has been everything and more. Him working away hasn't been as hard as I thought it would be. Sure I miss him but if Bryce and Hayden can do it, why can't we?

I think fate testing us like she has proves that we're meant to be.

Wanting to amp up our FaceTiming tonight, I quickly shower and slip into a sexy red nightgown. Not sure where it came from but I'm pretty sure it was a gag gift from Rani one Valentine's Day, but the gag's on her, I'm finally wearing it.

Pouring myself a glass of wine, I snuggle on the couch and wait for my man to call me. I laugh to myself when I realize that right now, I'm Netflix and chilling...by myself...waiting for my boyfriend to FaceTime me for sexy times. I snort out loud and spill my wine all over me.

Groaning, I shake my head, walk to my bedroom and change into sweats and a NY Crushers tank. I know I should support a Canadian team, being Canadian and all that, but when your brother is the goalie for them, it feels wrong rooting for anyone else...plus they are the best in the league.

With a new change of clothes, less sexy but comfier, I pour myself another glass of wine and laze back waiting for Hux to call.

The alarm on my phone blares and startles the shit out of me. I'm dazed and confused for a few seconds. Reaching to the side, I'm met with a soft cushion. Opening my eye, I see I'm still on the couch. My phone is still blaring on the coffee table, reaching over, I turn it off and deflate when I realize that he didn't do as he said. "He didn't call," I whisper.

My heart hurts that he didn't.

Picking up my phone, I click on the call log and see no missed call. I bring up my text messages and again, no text.

Standing up, I dejectedly head into my bedroom and get ready for work.

Not even wearing my favourite sky-high pumps puts a smile on my face, and clearly it's soured my attitude too because everyone is steering clear of me right now.

My phone rings, but it's an unknown number so I ignore it and get back to finalizing this report. I need to get it done ASAP because the big boss himself is flying in tomorrow. I'm bummed that Sully isn't joining him, but Harley has school, and she doesn't like to pull him out unnecessarily.

My phone rings again but this time, I see Bryce's name on the screen.

"Good afternoon, pretty lady."

"Kendall," she cries down the line.

"What's wrong?" I sit upright in my chair. My heart racing. Is it the baby? Hayden?

"It's...it's Westie..."

"What?" I screech like a banshee. Those in the cubicles outside my office all turn their heads and look toward me. "What about him?"

"He's in the hospital."

"What?" I scream again. By now, tears are cascading down my cheeks. My assistant, Vi, walks into my office. Her face scrunched in confusion. Bryce is explaining all that she knows but I'm not hearing her. All I keep thinking is that I'm a right royal bitchface for the things I was saying about him for not calling me last night like he promised.

"Kendall, you there?" Bryce yells, garnering my attention.

"I'm here," I tearfully say, "but I didn't hear anything you said, 'cause I was internally berating myself for being a bitchface."

"Why are you a bitchface?"

"Because I was mad he didn't call last night, but he didn't call cause he's in the hospital." I sit upright in my chair, "I need to get up to Kitimat."

"He's being airlifted back to Vancouver General."

"Okay, well, I'll go there then. I need to be there when he arrives and tell him I'm sorry for being a bitchface."

"Kendall, babe, he's in a coma."

"What?" I screech again. Leaning back in my chair, I

close my eyes and take a deep breath. "Okay, I'm listening now, tell me everything."

"I don't know the specifics, but he was hit with a valve thingy, he went flying and hit his head, and now he's sleeping. The thingy landed on his arm but it's all good in that he won't lose his arm. His mobility will be limited, but Westie is a stubborn bastard, he'll be fine."

Sitting here, I rapidly blink and process her words.

"Kendall, babe, you still there?"

Nodding my head, I swallow deeply and then I remember that she can't see me. "Yeah, no, I'm here. Just processing everything." I pause and focus on my desk. "I need to get to the hospital."

"I thought you'd want that so Hayden and I are on our way to your office to pick you up."

"How do you know where I work?"

"I know everything, Kendall Jones. Now, get your cute butt down to the lobby, we're almost there."

Nodding, I hang up.

"Everything okay?" Vi asks from my doorway.

Lifting my gaze to hers, when I see concern etched on her face, the tears begin to once again flow down my cheeks. "Huxley is in a coma and I'm a bitchface because I was angry he didn't call me last night, but he couldn't 'cause he was in the hospital. I'm the worst girlfriend ever."

"Oh, babe, I'm so sorry." Vi races into my office and around my desk. She pulls me up and envelops me in her arms. I wrap my arms around her and continue to cry. I haven't felt hurt like this since I heard about my grandparents' deaths.

A knock at my door startles us and we pull apart. When I look up, I see Bryce standing in the entrance to my office. "Bryce." I step around Vi and race over to her. She pulls me in for a hug and I start to blubber again. "Have you heard anything?" I tearfully mumble into her shoulder.

I feel her shake her head. "Not since we spoke." She grabs my upper arms and pushes me away. "Let's go see your man."

Nodding, I turn and look to Vi. "I've got this, and I'll call Hunter and explain what's happened."

"Thank you, Vi, you really are the best assistant."

"I know...just remember when bonus time comes around."

"Deal." I walk over to her and pull her in for another hug. "Thank you."

Picking up my handbag, I sling it over my shoulder and link arms with Bryce. We exit my office and head outside. Climbing into the back of their car, I sadly smile at Hayden.

"You okay?"

Shrugging my shoulders, I bite my bottom lip and stare at him. "I honestly don't know how I feel right now."

"That's understandable."

Bryce climbs into the front seat and looks toward her husband. "Let's get to the hospital and we can all get some peace of mind when we see Westie. Hopefully, by the time we get there, he'll be awake and flirting with the nurses." She looks back to me. "Sorry, but that's what he would have done if you weren't on the scene. He will see us walk in and he'll say something about me being fat. Then he'll beckon you to him and he'll slam his lips to yours and demand poutine."

"That's quite the scenario, Cookie."

"You can't tell me that that's not what you want to see when we walk in?"

"Well, no, I do want that. More than anything but..."

"But what?" I ask, leaning forward in my seat, waiting for his reply.

He sighs, "From what Troy said, he's gonna be out of it for a while."

From the back seat, I mumble, "This is bad, really, really bad." Choking back a sob, I cover my mouth and stare out the window.

As Hayden drives us to the hospital, I realize that my feelings for Huxley are much stronger than I thought. I know it's only been a short period of time, but I think I love him. It's crazy to be feeling like this so soon but when you know, you know. I really hope we get a chance to explore 'us' further but it seems that once again, fate is being a bitch.

27

HUXLEY

HAVE you ever been in a deep, deep sleep and then when you try and open your eyes it feels like you're eye lids are being weighed down? That's how I feel right now. No matter how much I try and open my eyes, I can't. My body feels fuzzy but heavy at the same time. Something isn't right but no matter what I do, I can't wake up.

I can hear people around me. Muttering and crying and in amongst all that there's this voice, it's angelic-like. It soothes me, and when I hear it, my body relaxes.

Drifting back into slumber and dreamland, I once again dream about kissing someone. Each time we kiss it's different but all the more intense. It's familiar but at the same time foreign.

Finally, I blink my eyes open and they stay open, but I quickly shut them because the light in the room is brighter than the sun. *"Turn the sun down,"* I think to myself. I can't voice my thoughts aloud because there's a tube down my throat. My eyes widen and I lift my hand, pulling at the tubes. My heart races because it feels weird and uncomfortable.

A soft hand touches mine and when I look over, I see a gorgeous brunette staring down at me. "Hey hey, leave it," she gently whispers. Leaning over me, she presses a button on the wall. She sits back on the edge of the bed and pulls my hand away from my face. "You're okay," she placates me and even though I don't know who she is, I feel calm and safe with her.

The door to my room swings open and a nurse walks in. "Welcome back," she states. She leans over and presses a button, a few moments later nurse after nurse enters my room, followed by a lady in a lab coat, who I'm guessing is my doctor. My angel, whoever she is, drops my hand and backs away, letting the doctor and nurses poke and prod me.

The doctor flashes a light in my eyes, blinding the fuck out of me. "Pupils reactive," she states with a smile. Pointing to my throat, she nods. "Okay, Huxley, we're going to remove your breathing tube. I'm going to need you to take a deep breath and then exhale. As you breathe out, I'm going to gently pull the tube down your throat out."

Nodding my head, she smiles in acknowledgement. "Okay, deep breath." I breathe in as she commands, and she begins to wriggle the tube. "And exhale." As I breathe out, she pulls the tube, and I can say it's the most uncomfortable feeling ever. The tube is free and I begin to cough. Holy fresh air, Batman, it feels good to breathe on my own right now, but fuck me sideways, my throat is burning.

As if sensing the burn, the brunette angel picks up the pitcher on the bed table and pours a glass. She pops a straw in and holds it to me.

Taking a sip, it feels like heaven when the cool liquid hits my throat. She pulls the cup away. "Not too much or you'll get sick." *I wonder if she's a nurse.*

"Are you my personal nurse?" I flirt with her, offering my best flirtatious smile. She laughs and smiles back, it lights her face up and my heart skips a beat. Before I can ask her anything else, the doctor asks her to leave.

She nods and exits my room, leaving me with my doctor and the nurses.

"How are you feeling, Huxley?"

"Like shit," I honestly tell her. My voice hoarse and my throat is dry and burning. I take the time to appraise my body, my arm is in a cast, which seems to be the only thing wrong, apart from the pounding in my head.

"With a bump to the head like you took, that's understandable."

"What happened?" I ask her because everything is foggy and jumbled.

"You were in an accident at work. Do you remember what you do?"

Nodding, I quickly stop as that hurts and the movement is making me queasy. "I'm a rig worker with Hayden."

"What else do you remember?" she probes me again.

"I...I..." Why is it so hard to answer this simple question?

"Can you tell me the last thing you remember?"

Her question stumps me, "I...umm, I don't really remember anything right now."

"Can you tell me your name?"

"Huxley Weston. I know my name and where I work, but the rest right now is all jumbled."

"Give yourself time to remember, don't force it." *Easier said than done,* I think to myself as I try to remember the accident and my life. "...now that you're awake I'll order another CT, and then we can go from there." I totally missed what the doctor said but she doesn't seem worried, so I guess I don't have anything to be worried about either.

She and the nurses exit my room, leaving me alone with my jumbled thoughts.

The door to my room opens again and this time, Hayden enters with two chicks, one being my brunette angel. "Good to see you awake, Sleeping Beauty," he teases. "How you feelin dude?"

"Feel like I've been asleep for days and hit with a sledgehammer."

"Well, you have kinda been asleep for days and as for a sledgehammer, replace it with a valve."

My eyes widen at his words. "Hayden, don't." One of the women berates him. My gaze flicks between the three of them. I stare intently at the two women standing next to him. One is pregnant, well, I think pregnant, but I know never to mention that because twenty times out of ten, they aren't and are just fat. The other chick is the most beautiful woman I've ever seen in my life. Brown waves hang loose around her shoulders. Her eyes are bloodshot but they are the richest of brown in colour, reminding me of liquid chocolate. She's not saying anything, she's just staring at me, looking relieved that I'm awake.

My brows furrow because I cannot place her so finally, I ask, "Who are you?"

"WHO ARE YOU? NICE ONE, WESTIE," Bryce laughs. She steps to his side, bends down and hugs him. From my spot near the door, I see his eyes widen. Part of me is hoping he's playing a trick but from the blank expression on his face, he really doesn't know who we are. He's *not* joking with us.

"Bryce," Hayden says, rubbing her back. She's still hugging Huxley and he's getting antsy at the contact. "Bryce," Hayden says louder, he pulls on her arm, finally garnering her attention.

She stands up and pulls her arm free. Spinning to face him, she glares at him and I kinda feel sorry for him right now. "Hayden Bowden, do not 'Bryce' me right now. If I want to hug him, I will hug him and—" She stops mid-sentence when she sees the stern and concerned look on her husband's face. "What?"

"Dude, this chick just scolded you. If you don't lock her down, you're a fool."

Bryce spins around to face Huxley, her mouth

opening and closing in shock. Her eyes wide like saucers. "You...you really have no clue who I am?" she asks, her voice high-pitched and strained right now. He shakes his head side to side, wincing from the action. "What about her?" She flicks her thumb over to me.

He looks around her and over to me. He stares at me. His eyes are locked on mine, and I wish with everything I have that the next words out of his mouth are my name, but before he even opens his mouth, I know he has no idea who I am from the blank and confused expression on his face.

"I have no idea who she is." With another shake of his head, he looks at Bryce and back to me again. Each time, no recognition flickers in his gaze.

My eyes well with tears, hearing it again hurts just as much as hearing it the first time. He looks at me and when I see the blank look reflecting back at me, I shatter on the inside. Fate has once again fucked us over, proving once and for all, fairy tales and happily ever afters are bullshit.

His gaze darts between Hayden and me. "Who are you?" he asks again.

Who are you?

Three words that obliterate my heart.

Nine letters that cut me deeper than ever before.

"Stop messing with us, Huxley Weston," Bryce scolds him.

"I wish I was, but I literally do not know you two chicks."

Her eyes widen and her face drops when she finally

realizes that he isn't messing with her. "You really don't know us?"

He shakes his head, again wincing from the motion. "I'm sorry, I don't."

"Well, what's the last thing you remember?" I ask, shocking myself that I can even speak because I'm broken right now, absolutely heartbroken that the man I love doesn't know me.

My eyes pop wide open when I realize that yes, I do love him, no more thinking I do like I did in the car earlier. I love Huxley Weston...and he doesn't even know who I am.

HUXLEY

"EXCUSE ME," she tearfully says. We all turn and watch as she opens the door and runs out of my room. An audible sob can be heard just before the door clicks shut.

I stare at the door, not sure what I'm expecting right now. All I know is that I think I just broke that girl's heart. "I think I just broke that girl," I mumble.

"Ya think?" the woman I now know as Bryce snaps at me.

"Bryce," Hayden warns her.

"No, I just," she raises her hand in a stop motion at him, "no. I'm just, gah." She throws her hands up in frustration, shaking her head. Before he can say anything, she races out of the room. "Kendall," I hear her shout, just before the door clicks shut.

"Kendall," I whisper to myself. I like the way her name sounds inside my head, looking to Hayden, I rub the back of my neck. "What am I missing here?" I ask him.

"What do you mean?"

"Kendall? Bryce? What the hell, man?"

"You really have no clue? You're not fucking with us?"

"Seriously, no clue who those chicks are."

Hayden squeezes the back of his neck. "Bryce is my wife."

"Wife?" I shout. "How—"

"How what?"

"How are you married? You...you're single. I'm single. We're ready to mingle."

"Dude, Bryce and I have been married for nearly two years now and she's having our baby in December."

"What the fuck?" Have I been unconscious for all that? "How long have I been out for?"

"Three days."

"But you've been married for nearly two years. How the fuck does that all work? I don't understand any of this."

"What do you last remember?"

"Flying to Alberta for a new gig with you."

"Dude, that was five years ago."

Shaking my head, I stare at the waffle weave blanket covering my legs. Lifting my head up, I stare over at my friend. "But we just started with Troy in Alberta."

"No," he sternly says, "that was five years ago."

"What the fuck else have I missed?"

"I, umm, I don't know how much I should tell you. The movies say to let it come back organically."

"This isn't a fucking movie, Hayden, this is my life. A life that I seem to be missing five years of right now."

Slamming my fist down on the bed, I groan in frustration, "Fuuuuck." I slam it down again. "This is fucked up."

"Yep," he agrees. Dragging the chair from near the window, he slides it next to the bed and takes a seat next to me. "What can I do to help?"

30

KENDALL

I CAN'T BE HERE, this, it's all too much to handle right now. "Excuse me," I tearfully tell everyone. Turning on my heel, I exit the room and race down the corridor.

Just as I turn the corner, I hear Bryce yell out, "Kendall, babe, wait up."

Reaching the end of the corridor, I turn and lean against the wall. Covering my mouth, I swallow down the lump in the back of my throat just as Bryce joins me.

"Are you okay?" she asks. Reaching out, she takes my hand in hers and squeezes.

"Yes. No. I don't know." Dropping my head, I close my eyes and sigh. Biting my lip, I lift my head and stare at Bryce. "How are you with all of this?"

"It hurts like hell that he doesn't remember me, but it also means he forgets all the dumb shit I've done so, silver lining."

I laugh at that, then feel guilty for laughing because I have my memories and feelings. "I never told him I loved him, and I do," I tearfully tell her. "I should have been honest with him, even though I only realized just now that I do, but still, I should have..." A sob breaks free and I slide down the wall. My ass hits the linoleum and I break down. Resting my head on my knees, I cry my broken heart out.

"I'm sure with time he'll remember it all, we just have to think positive." Bryce says but from the tone of her voice, I can tell she doesn't one hundred percent believe what she's saying.

Lifting my head, I tearfully stare up at Bryce. "How can the man I love not remember me? How?"

After my meltdown, Bryce takes me down to the cafeteria and she treats me to a shitty coffee and a Butterfinger. "I really wish this was a cosmo," I tell her, wincing on my sip of black sludge.

"At least you can drink cosmos."

"At least you won't get hungover from said cosmo."

"At least you don't get heartburn from drinking water. Or need to pee every two point five seconds."

"Wow, pregnancy sounds great."

"Oh, it's the best," she excitedly replies. "That first time Hayd and I saw our munchkin on the screen, everything was right in the world." She continues to talk about the wonders and joys of being pregnant. She's so happy and excited, and I'm happy for her, I really am...even if my world just imploded with the uttering of three words. Three insignificant words, but together in a sentence they had the power to destroy me.

We make our way back up to Huxley's door. I stop in the hallway across from the man I love's hospital room, and I look to Bryce. "Do I go in? Or do I go home? What's the protocol when someone you love doesn't know you?"

"What do you want to do?"

"I want to stay. I want him to know I'm here, even if he doesn't remember me, but I also don't want to make him uncomfortable. What's the etiquette here?"

"I don't think there is one but if it was Hayden in that bed, I'd be in there doing everything I could to get him to remember me."

"What if he never remembers me?"

"What if he does?" she throws back at me. "And if he doesn't, make him fall in love with you all over again."

"He doesn't love me."

She nods. "Yeah, he does."

"But he never said it."

"Neither did you."

"Touché."

We silently stare at one another outside the hospital room of the man who currently has no clue who either one of us is.

"So, what's it gonna be? You gonna walk away? Or are you going to make him fall in love with you all over again?"

My lips lift into a grin. "I'm gonna get my man to love me again."

31

HUXLEY

"WHAT CAN I DO TO HELP?" My best friend asks me, and I know he will do anything to help me because if the shoe was on the other foot, I'd be doing everything in my power to help him too.

"Do you happen to have a magic sword that you can wave and bobbity-bibbidy-boop and then I'll remember?"

"The saying is actually bibbity-bobbity-boo, and the fairy godmother uses a wand, not a sword, but seeing her wave a sword around could be pretty awesome too," a soft voice from the doorway says. Turning my attention away from Hayden, I smile when I see the hottie from before. I stare at her intently but for the life of me, I don't know who she is.

She must sense my hesitation because she walks over to me and offers her hand. "Hi, I'm Kendall."

As soon as her hand touches mine, a jolt of electricity zaps up my arm. I hope it will jolt my brain but it doesn't, apart from an intense sexual spark, nothing.

"Westie," I reply.

"I've mostly known you as Huxley, only recently did I discover you're also known as Westie."

"And how do we know one another?"

Hayden snorts. "Oh, boy, that's a story and a half but as I was just saying, I think you need to let it come back to you organically."

Kendall sucks in a breath at his words, he looks to Kendall and shrugs. "I'm sorry, but it's what I think."

"What do the doctors say?" she asks me, ignoring Hayden and his weird 'let-him-remember-on-his-own' suggestion. Her tone is laced with concern, alluding to me that we're something special to each other.

"I haven't spoken to them yet about it."

"Well, until we get a clear direction, I'm happy to leave it as me just being Kendall, the girl you don't know." Those last words are laced with sadness. She looks directly at me and I can feel her stare deep in my soul but at the same time, it feels blank and unknow. "You need to look after you right now, Hux." She smiles but it doesn't reach her eyes. I may not remember this woman, but I know that what she just said is complete and utter horse-shit. She's devastated that I don't remember who she is, and to be honest, I hate that I don't know her either.

32

KENDALL

...three weeks later

IT'S BEEN three weeks and three days since I got that fateful call from Bryce and the last three weeks have sucked donkey dick. Huxley still doesn't remember me. His moods are up and down like a roller coaster, and it looks like he won't be able to return to work doing what he loves. The valve that landed on him has limited the mobility in his left arm, and he can no longer swing off tag lines, whatever the hell those are. He's turned into Mr. Grumpy Pants ever since getting that news. Snapping at everyone, he even made Bryce cry the other day, but then again, she cries at the drop of a hat at the moment due to her raging pregnancy hormones.

I hate not being able to help him get through all of this. The memory loss is bad enough, add his job loss into the equation and it's epically shit.

I spend most of my evenings at the hospital, mostly in silence because I don't know what to say without him getting angry. I'm starting to wonder if I should stay away. However, the thought of not being near him is unfathomable. I can't explain it but I just need to be near him. I'm slowly falling behind at work, hence why I'm heading in at stupid a.m.

The sky is still dark and the sun is not even close to poking its head above the horizon, but I couldn't lie in bed staring at the ceiling any longer. When I step out onto the floor, my face scrunches in confusion because there's a light on in my office and I see shadows. Security never mentioned that someone was up here so I'm on high alert.

Cautiously, I walk down the corridor, I hear a female giggle, which confuses me even more. Opening the door to my office, I poke my head in and my mouth drops open when I see Sully straddling Hunter's lap on my sofa. My eyes connect with Hunter's and his widen in shock. Sully is lost to the pleasure and doesn't notice the change in Hunter. Before he can let her know I'm here, she screams out as her orgasm takes over. Before she's finished, she climbs off his lap and lowers her head. He pushes on her shoulders and from the pained expression on his face, he isn't too happy at being interrupted.

"Umm, babe, as much as I'd love to finish what we started, we have company." He head nods toward a frozen me.

She turns her head and when she sees me, her face turns beet red. "Oh, my fucking god," she screeches in a mortified tone. Dropping her head into Hunter's crotch, he groans.

"Umm, babe," he hisses through clenched teeth, her

head precariously close to his dick—which I thankfully cannot see because no one wants to see their boss's junk, no matter how hot he is.

"I'll give you five," I quickly say.

Spinning on my heel, I race out of my office and down to the restrooms. Pushing the door open, I step inside, lean on the counter, and lower my head. Sucking in a deep breath, I lift my head and stare at my reflection. Tears are welled in my eyes, and before I can stop them, the first one falls. Staring at myself, I begin to break down and cry.

The door opens and I lower my head in embarrassment, quickly wiping the liquid on my face. "K, babe, I'm so sorry you saw that, our flight got in early, and Harley is with Papa Crawford, so we came down to get an early start and then—oh, God, you walked in and now I...wait. Are you crying?"

"No," I tearfully reply.

Turning my head, I stare at her through the tears that just won't stop. They continue to cascade down my cheeks. She gives me her 'mom look' so I nod. "Yesssss, I'm crying," I blubber.

"No shit," she says. Then she opens her arms and walks toward me. "Oh, babe, come here." We step to one another and she envelops me in her arms, giving me the mom hug that I really, really need right now. As soon as I'm in her mom embrace, I break down further. I let out everything that I've been holding in for the last three weeks.

She pulls back and holds on to my upper arms. "What's wrong? Surely, Hunter's junk didn't scare you that much. I know it's big, but Harley came out of my hoo-ha, therefore a big cock is nothing, well, it's not nothing, but...oh, crap, I'm waffling again. What's wrong? Has something happened with Huxley?"

"You mean apart from the man I love still not remembering me?"

"Still no recognition?"

Shaking my head, I swipe at the tears on my cheeks. "Nope, nothing. I don't know if my being there is helping or hindering right now. I want to be close to him so that maybe it will spark some memory of me, of us. I want to help him but I'm helpless to do that. He doesn't even remember us Netflix and chilling. How can it all be gone?"

"K, when's the last time you slept properly?"

Pursing my lips, I think over her question. "Ummm..."

"And why are you coming to the office at stupid a.m.?"

"Because I'm behind with the summer marketing plan and I need to get it prepped to present to Hunter and Conrad next month."

"Fuck the marketing plan, you need to look after you...and Huxley."

"I also need a job."

"Your job is safe, K. You are one of the best marketing coordinators that Luxe has, Hunter will be a dickwad if he fires you, plus I know you, I bet that plan is just about finalized."

"Maybe," I throw back at her with a shoulder shrug,

then out of nowhere I ask, "Why were you two getting jiggy with it in my office?"

"It was a spur-of-the-moment thing."

"You do realize we're in a hotel and your partner owns said hotel and has access to any room he wants." She shrugs at me. "Just spur elsewhere next time."

"I love that you say next time, it's like you know me so well."

"Yes, yes, I do know you well. I don't know how many times I walked in on you two when I was in Hawaii last year."

"We had five years to make up for," she nonchalantly replies with a shrug and a wink.

"That's how long of a gap his memory is. What if he never remembers?"

"What if he does? And if he doesn't, you just need to make him fall for you again."

"This isn't a fairy tale. This is real life and another slap in the face that fairy tales are shit. I'm just not destined to get my happily ever after."

"Trust me, you'll get your HEA, if I got mine, you too will get yours."

Not wanting to keep focusing on the shitshow that is my forgetful love life, I change the topic. "Let's get out of the restroom and focus on work." Linking arms with her, we exit and head back to my office. The time for wallowing is over. I need to get back to work and focus.

"So, in order for this to happen we need..." I rattle off all that I need to finalize for my meeting next month.

"Wow, you really are bossy when you're not getting

laid," she interrupts me on my list-making rant as we continue down the hallway to my office.

"Please, don't remind me. I'm getting buzz burn—"

"Aaaaand, that's my cue to leave," Hunter says from the doorway to my office.

"Oh.My.God, can this day get any more mortifying?" I totally forgot he was in here waiting for us. My mind is a jumbled mess right now. If my head wasn't screwed on, I think I would have lost it weeks ago.

"Maybe," Sully replies cheekily, "it is only 5 a.m."

Thankfully, the rest of the day was smooth sailing and there were no more 'incidents' as such. Today was also the first time in three weeks that I didn't go to the hospital after work. It felt odd not going, but after chatting with Sully and Hunter over lunch it seems like a good idea...I think.

Hunter's train of thought is that me not being there will spark something in Huxley. At first, Sully thought it was a 'fucking stupid idea' and told Hunter to 'shut his face.' Much to her disgust, I agreed with him and his 'absence makes the heart grow fonder' mantra. Sully thinks that saying is complete horseshit, but what do I have to lose? It's not like he can forget me again, right?

So, instead of going to the hospital, I went home, changed into my running gear, and went for a run. Something I haven't done in a very long time. It was just what I needed to clear the mind and reinvigorate myself.

And for the last few days, that's exactly what I've done.

Work.

Home.

Run.

Repeat.

On day four, there's a knock at my office door and when I look up, I see Bryce and Hayden standing there. "Hey," I offer in greeting and stand up, walking around my desk. I hug them both and offer them my sofa...which I got dry-cleaned two days ago, after catching my boss and friend together on it.

"Don't hey me, miss," Bryce snarls as she sits down, resting her hands on her growing belly. "You haven't been to the hospital."

"I'm giving him space."

"Space schmace," she replies. "How can he remember you if you're not there?"

"Hunter and—"

"Who the fuck is Hunter?"

"That'd be me," his deep voice says from the doorway, startling us all.

"You've moved on already?" Bryce asks me, her voice cracking on the word already.

"No," I quickly refute, "Hunter is the CEO of Luxe, he and Sully are here visiting from Hawaii and...and I'm going back with them."

"You're leaving?" Hayden questions, "What about Westie?"

"I just...I need to get away. It's too hard not having him remember me. Hunter thinks my absence will make him remember."

"And it's fucking stupid if you ask me," Sully says, barging into my office. She looks to Bryce and Hayden. "I'm Sully, or Krista, and this is my boo, Hunter." He rolls his eyes at her referring to him as 'her boo' and I can't help but laugh.

"Your boo, that's too cute."

"Don't make me fire you," Hunter teasingly says, pulling Sully into his side and gazing down at her lovingly.

"You won't," I sassily throw back at my boss, "according to 'your boo' I'm too valuable."

"Well, you are but don't tempt me."

The room falls silent and as I look around my office, I realize I'm the only single one in here. Seeing all the couples hurts because I could be one of them, but the man I love has no fucking clue who I am. The first tear slides down my cheek, I wipe at my cheek but I can't stop the avalanche of tears falling. "Why doesn't he remember me?" I blubber. "I just, I can't be around him and not have him remember us. It hurts too much." I sniff unlady-like. "I just don't think I'm meant to get my happily ever after like you four."

"You are full of shit, Kendall Jones," Sully informs me.

"I agree with Sully," Bryce adds. "The path to any HEA is never smooth, you guys are just going through the motions."

"But—"

"No buts," Bryce interrupts. She shimmies closer to me, reaches over, and takes my hand in hers. "I will allow you to go to Hawaii but my golly gosh, girlie, you better come back and when you do, you and Westie will get your HEA. You two are meant to be."

"How do you know?"

"Call it mother's intuition."

"You're so full of crap."

"Don't verbally abuse a pregnant woman,"

"That's a bit much, Cookie," Hayden adds, rubbing Bryce's back.

"No, it's not. I just know they're meant to be." Her eyes well with tears, "I just want them happy like us." She begins to cry now. "Stupid pregnancy hormones make me so emotional."

Hayden quietly mumbles, "And irrational." And luckily for him, his wife doesn't hear him.

"Are you gonna be like this when we have another?" Hunter asks. "All emotional and crazy?" He looks to Bryce. "Sorry, no offence."

"It's fine," she tearfully replies, "and yes, she will." She wipes at her face and suddenly, happy determined Bryce is back. She looks intently at me. "Okay, so, you go to Hawaii, come back with a killer tan, and then we win back your man."

I nod in agreement. "Yep." I let the 'p' pop and wonder if she's right. Will I be able to get Huxley to remember me and fall in love with me again?

33

HUXLEY

I'M bored out of my mind, I cannot wait to be sprung free from this joint, but according to the doctors, that's not happening for a few more days yet. Seems being in a coma and the memory loss is kind of a big deal. Combined with a wonky arm and the extra surgeries, I get it, but I just want my own bed, a decent meal, and an ice-cold beer. The food here is shit, epically shit. The coffee is shit, and don't get me started on the bed. How are people meant to recover sleeping on a lump of shit like this?

The only thing I look forward to is my daily visit from that Kendall girl, even if I have no memory of her. After me begging, Hayden finally told me how I know her. It explains her sadness when I first woke up and the hopeful look in her eye each time she visits, but she's a stranger to me.

She hasn't been by in a few days, and even though I don't remember her, I'm missing her.

Each day we sit here quietly and watch Netflix. The

other day she made a joke about Netflix and chilling, but it went straight over my head, and the look of utter defeat on her face hurt me just as much as I apparently hurt her. And now I think about it, that was the day before she stopped visiting me. Maybe my memory loss has become too much for her. I know it's pissing me off, I can only imagine how she feels.

"How's my favourite patient doing?" Leah, my evening nurse, asks, striding into my room. She picks up my chart and reads over it and smiles at me. She's always so bright and bubbly.

"Still memoryless," I reply...like I do each time she asks.

"That just means there's more room to make new memories."

"But what if my old memories are good memories?"

"What if they're not?"

"Are you always this chipper?"

"Yep," she replies with a shrug. "Now, when's the last time you showered?"

"Are you wanting to get me naked?" I tease.

"You have the wrong bits for my liking, but I can appreciate a fine male specimen so sure, get your gear off."

"You're gay?"

She lifts her left hand and wiggles her ring finger at me. "Happily married since two thousand and five."

"Well, good for you. I'm still looking for my princess."

"I think you've already found her."

"Huh?" I deadpan, confused because I don't have a someone special.

"The girl who's always here."

"Kendall?"

"That's the one, she looks at you with stars in her eyes. She reminds me so much of my wife, in the way she looks at you."

"She does not look at me like that."

"Men are so dense sometimes, that girl has it bad for you."

"But I don't know her. Well, I don't remember her." Shaking my head, I sigh. "How do I not remember the one I supposedly love?"

"The brain works in mysterious ways, Huxley. One day you'll be doing something completely random and then BAM all your memories will come flooding back to you."

"But what if they don't?"

"You make new ones." She pats my arm and turns to walk out of my room but before she leaves, she looks over her shoulder at me. "You know what to do if you need anything from me."

Before I can reply, Leah exits my room, leaving me alone with an empty head and an aching heart. For the rest of the evening, I keep playing her words over and over in my head, 'make new ones'. Is it that easy though?

34

KENDALL

"YOU SURE THAT'S what you want to do?" Kallen asks me as I walk toward the hospital.

"I don't know anything anymore. Hunter thinks my not being here will spark something—"

"Absence makes the heart grow fonder type shit."

"Yeah, Sully thinks I'm being a moron and need to be here in his face to remember, but I can't do that anymore. It hurts not having him remember."

"I should just deck him like I promised to do if he ever hurt you."

"You're going to deck a man who has no memory? That's a dick move."

"Well, I need to do something."

"You need to keep your head down and train your heart out so you can take the Crushers all the way to the Cup, again. I won't be happy if you fuck up my team's streak." Even though it's a team sport, I blame Kallen for any loss that my precious Crushers have.

"Please, they hired me because I'm the best goalie in the NHL."

"Someone's full of themselves...but Kal, I'm so freakin' proud of you, following your dream like you have."

"Aww, thanks, Sis. I'm proud of you too."

"Just don't fuck my team up."

"We've won the last few years, well except for last year but that wasn't my fault, that was all on Douchmen."

"He really lives up to the moniker of his Däuchmen last name, doesn't he?"

Kal laughs, "he sure does." And then we fall silent. "How are the rents?"

"Same old, same old."

"So, being selfish dicks and doing their own thing?"

"Pretty much." I pause and start thinking about Pops and Nanna. "I miss them," I quietly add.

"Me too," he agrees and then chuckles. "You know, Pops would kick Huxley's ass if he was still alive. He'd say, 'How can you forget an angel like my Kendall?' and then he'd research injuries like his, doing all he could to help get his memories of you back."

"And Nanna would fuss all over him and she'd somehow pull his memories of me out." My eyes well with tears. I take a seat on a bench outside the hospital. "They would have loved him," I tearfully whisper to Kal, and then quietly add, "like I still do."

"Are you crying?" he asks me.

"No," I say, followed by a sniff.

"That sniff says otherwise."

"It's just allergies."

"Bullshit...are you sure you don't want me to fly up?"

"No, I'm flying to Hawaii tomorrow."

"Nice, maybe Chels and I will come visit you there. Get a holiday in before training starts in September."

"If you get a chance before training starts, that would be great, but DO NOT," I place emphasis on the two words, "fuck up—"

"My team. Got it. I love you, Sis."

"I love you too, baby bro."

Hanging up from my brother, I walk into the hospital. Standing in the hallway outside of Huxley's hospital room, I stare at the door, willing myself to put my hand on the handle, open it, and step inside. I need to say goodbye before I fly out early tomorrow morning.

I've never felt so torn before. A part of me wants to be here and help him remember, but there's also a part of me that's angry he doesn't remember me. We had a connection, a strong one that started on New Year's Eve and with one valve that connection, and all his memories, were severed.

"You can go in, you know," Leah, the night shift nurse, tells me.

"I know, I'm just..."

"Here to say goodbye?"

My head snaps toward her. "How did you know?"

"Because every other day you've waltzed in all gung-ho and had a smile that could light a small village on your face, and today, well, today you look like your dog just died."

"I think my imaginary dog dying would be easier to

deal with than the man I love not remembering who I am."

"So, you do love him?"

"I do but..."

"He just needs time to remember."

"Everyone keeps saying that, but what if he never remembers me? What if the new Huxley doesn't want me? I don't think I could handle that rejection; this is hard enough as it is."

"And it's just as hard for him," she reminds me. I hate that she's right but I think, for now, I need to look after me. Maybe Hunter is right and the space will make him remember.

"I know that, but what if my being here is making it harder for him, I think it's for the best that I go to Hawaii for work." I swallow the lump building in my throat. "For him to get better I need to go. And, and for me, I need to let him go."

The door to his room swings open and Huxley is standing in the doorway, the look on his face is murderous. "Then by all means, go," he angrily snaps, I've never seen him like this before.

"Huxley, I—"

"Save it. I don't need or want your pity. I don't even know who you are. Just leave. You live your life and I'll live mine."

He slams the door in my face. I stand here and stare at the closed door. My already torn heart shatters further.

"He doesn't mean that." Leah squeezes my shoulder. "An outburst like that is common with memory loss."

"His outbursts are getting worse, and they seem to

only happen so severely when I'm here," I sniff. "This outburst now confirms that it's for the best if I go."

Resting my palm flat on his door, I whisper, "Good-bye, Hunky Huxley."

Sadly smiling at Leah, I turn on my heel and leave. With each step I take away from him, I wonder if I'm making a mistake.

35

HUXLEY

SLAMMING the door shut in her face, I stare at the wood and shake my head. Clearly, she didn't love, like, whatever we were, enough to stick around. But then again, why would anyone stick by me? My mom didn't want me. My dad, who the fuck knows where he is. The only constants in my life are Hayden, Troy, and my job. And now not even that's safe. My career, and life, are effectively over due to this accident.

Shuffling back to my bed, I sink down on the lump they call a mattress and stare at my toes. Maybe I should just end it all now, and then everyone will move on and I won't be a burden on anyone anymore.

Falling to my back, I stare up at the ceiling and know that I won't end it. I'm too stubborn to do that, plus if I did, Hayden would miss me too much. And according to Bryce, I'm going to live 'til I'm a hundred and seven, with my wife and seven kids. Not sure where she got that crazy idea from, but I do want the wife and kids thing. I just need to find a wife first.

There's a knock at my door and then it opens. "Avon calling," Hayden singsongs, stepping into my room.

Looking up, I nod at him in greeting and sit up. "No wife tonight?" I ask, it's so weird saying that because in my memory, he's single.

"She's chatting with Kendall, we bumped into her on the way in. She's off to Hawaii for work tomorrow."

"I heard," I snap at him.

"Have I missed something?" he asks me, and I honestly don't know how to answer. I'm saved from answering when Bryce waddles in, but from the look on her face, suddenly, I'd rather have that conversation with Hayden.

"Huxley Jeremiah Weston, you are a dickwad asshole. How could you?"

"How could I what?" I ask, confused.

"Be such a dickwad asshole to Kendall just now?"

"Huh?"

"She's been nothing but supportive and loving and hoping that you will get your memories back. She's been here every day, working herself to the bone between coming here and work, and then when she comes to tell you she's leaving you turn into a dickwad asshole."

"Hold your fucking horses, lady—"

"Dude, don't speak to my wife like that."

"But it's okay for her to repeatedly call me a dickwad asshole and lay into me over something she knows nothing about..."

"I know what happened. Kendall just told me. You broke her, Huxley."

"But she's leaving."

"For work, you dickwad asshole."

"Will you stop with the dickwad asshole?"

"If the dickwad asshole fits, I'll use it. Just tell me one thing, why?"

"Why what?"

"Why did you explode like that?"

"Because everyone leaves."

"She's coming back, you idiot, and FYI; the world doesn't revolve around you. Kendall is a person and needs time too. Do you think it's easy for her to have the man she loves not remember her?"

"Well, no, it's all-around shit."

"Exactly, but instead of being an adult about it you acted like—"

"A dickwad asshole."

"Exactly." She huffs. "Now, how are you going to fix it?"

Shrugging my shoulders, I sigh. "I don't know. I just want my memories back. I want to be able to go back to work." I pause. "I want my life back."

"And you will, Westie. You just need to give it time, but you need to stop taking it out on everyone."

"Bryce is right dude plus, you're too stubborn to lose them forever," Hayden adds, lightening the heaviness of the mood in the room. "But there might be a few things you want to forget...like this one time..."

"I don't want to hear any antics from the two of you before I came along."

"Who said it was before you came along?" he teases his wife, and from the look on her face right now, I think he'll be sleeping on the couch tonight.

"Duuuude, don't poke Momma Bear, she's scary when she's angry."

"You should listen to him, dear husband."

"Yes, wife," Hayden coos like the lovesick fool he is.

"I don't remember you, but you really are perfect for him, Bryce. And that kid," I point to her belly, "is going to be lucky to have you both as parents."

Bryce starts to cry. "Westie, that's so sweet of you to say." She sniffs in a really unladylike way. "And he or she will have a kick-ass uncle in you."

"Hell yeah, he will."

"It could be a she."

"Nah, boy...I'm feeling a boy and by the way, Huxley is a fantabulous name."

"One Huxley is enough," Hayden adds, "even if you are a dickwad asshole sometimes."

Flipping him the bird, I shake my head. "Speaking of me being a dickwad asshole, I think I need to apologize to Kendall."

"Yes. Yes, you do," Bryce agrees. "Now, I need food or I'm going to become hangry."

"Become hangry, I think you already are. The way you laid into me just now was scary."

"And don't you forget it," she states matter-of-factly with a scowl. "I look after my family, Huxley, and when one hurts, we all hurt."

How she is being so nice to me when I was a mega dickwad asshole is beyond me, but I guess we are close, and family. I may be missing the last five years, but I think she's right, she and Hayden are my family...and possibly Kendall too, but I think I blew that.

"Bryce, do you umm, ahh, have Kendall's number?"

"It's in your phone."

Picking up my phone, I bring up her contact. My finger hovers over it but at the last minute, I decide to text her instead.

> **HUXLEY:** *Hi, Kendall. It's Huxley. I need to apologize for being such a dickwad asshole earlier. I shouldn't take my frustrations out on those who are trying to help me. Anyway, good luck in Hawaii and again, I'm sorry. Cheers, Huxley.*

Throwing my phone back onto the bed table, I lie back down, but it beeps and all three of us stare at it.

> **KENDALL:** *Thanks for the apology but for now, I think it's best if I stay away...even if I wasn't going away for work. I hope you get your memories back, Hux. Kendall Xo*

I deflate when I read her message, but I also understand. I know I'd hate it if the person I loved suddenly stopped remembering me. It feels like there's a hole in my heart now, but how can that be when I have no recollection of who Kendall Jones is?

36

KENDALL

...five weeks later

I'M FLYING BACK from Hawaii today, and I have an overnight layover in Seattle, normally that would piss me off but I'm excited for it. One, I've never been to Seattle, and two, to be honest, I don't think I'm quite ready to return to Vancouver. To be in the same city as Huxley and have him still not remember me is going to be torture. Being in the same city and not seeing him will also be an adjustment, but it's for the best...I need to look after myself and my heart.

Getting away was just what I needed. I enjoyed it so much, I stayed for five weeks instead of two like I had originally planned. I'm so glad I decided to get away. For the last week, Sully has reminded me daily how awesome her suggestion was, even though it was Hunter who suggested it and not her.

I don't think about Huxley as much as when I first left Vancouver but I'll be doing something completely random, and it will remind me of him, and the hurt hits me like a freight train and I'm back to square one again.

I've been keeping in touch with Bryce. She told me that he was discharged from the hospital just after I left and that he's currently living with them. She didn't want him living on his own with his memory, or lack thereof.

She said he's slowly remembering things but I'm not one of them. I'm not sure he will ever remember me so I've decided that I'm going to cut ties with him. That revelation came about one night after having waaaaay too many cosmos with Sully at a local bar...

...*"That guy over there is checking you out,"* Sully *informs me as she places another pitcher of cosmos on the table between us. We are three sheets to the wind drunk right now, and it's nice to feel numb from alcohol rather than heartbreak.*

My heart hurts for Huxley just as much now as it did the day I left. I haven't heard from him since his apology text, and I don't know if that's a good thing or not.

"That's nice," I reply, picking up my glass and taking a sip.

"Really? You're not even going to look?"

"Nope, not interested. I don't need or want a man."

"He's really hot."

"Don't let Hunter hear you say that."

"He and I are allowed to browse the food court, we just need to dine at home."

"You two are fucking weird."

She nonchalantly shrugs. We spend the next ten minutes discussing who's hotter between Captain

America and Thor. FYI, it's Thor because hello, an Aussie accent.

She looks at me over her drink and I just know that she's going to broach the Huxley subject. "So, Huxley." BINGO, *I think to myself. "What are you going to do about the situation with him?"*

"Wow, way to go for the jugular." Picking up my drink, I drain what's left and top my glass up.

"Babe, it's been four weeks now, and you haven't mentioned him once in that time, and it's starting to drive me fucking crazy not knowing what you plan on doing when you go home."

"I plan on living my life."

"Without him?"

"Yep." She looks at me with an expression of shock on her face. "He doesn't remember me, Sul. I need to move on, like I'm sure he has."

"I guarantee you he hasn't moved on." She pauses, and then tacks on. "One day he might remember you again."

"And he might not. What if Huxley two point zero doesn't want me? I couldn't take that rejection. This is hard enough as it is."

"But—"

"Nope," I shake my head, "no buts. Huxley and I had our moment and clearly he isn't my forever."

"I think you're giving up too easily but I'll leave it alone."

"Thank you."

"But before I do, just think about seeing him again. One last time."

"*Nope, not happening. I should have known that Huxley and I weren't meant to be. Look at the hiccups with us to begin with. Fate clearly has another plan.*"

"*Fuck fate and her plan. Hunter and I are the perfect case of that.*"

"*But you and Hunter are meant to be.*"

"*As are you and Huxley.*"

"*Nope, our story is over. We reached our end and there was no happily ever after for us. He will live his life, and I'll live mine...separately.*"

...since making that decision, I feel like I'm on the path to happiness again. I still have my down days, but I know with time my heart will heal. For that to happen, I need to get back to Vancouver and start living again, but first, I'm going to explore Seattle.

I spend a wonderful day roaming around Seattle. The main thing I wanted to visit was the Space Needle and it really didn't disappoint. It's a very pretty city and I'd love to come back and explore it some more.

I'm currently in an Uber on my way back to the airport. My adventure has come to an end and it's time to return to the real world. For a fleeting moment, I wonder if Huxley will want to see me when I return but I push that aside. The Huxley chapter in my life is over. I need to move on and forget all about Hunky Huxley and his magical pierced tongue.

After checking in, I head toward a coffee shop in need of a caffeine boost plus coffee, hello. I'm shattered after my day exploring. Waiting in line, I look around the terminal when the hairs on the back of my neck prickle, someone races past the coffee shop, and a feeling of déjà vu washes over me. He turns his head, and our gaze meets through the frosted glass. I can't actually see his eyes, but I just know we're staring at one another. Everything around me fades away. It's just him and me but within the blink of an eye, he's gone and that prickly feeling disappears.

I can't shake the feeling that I've been in this situation before but seriously, if I blinked, I would have missed him. *Maybe I imagined him?* I think to myself while I wait to order my coffee.

Reaching the counter, I place my order and step to the waiting area. I keep looking out into the terminal, hoping to see my mystery man but he's gone.

With my coffee in hand, I walk through the terminal toward my boarding gate. My head is down, looking in my bag for my phone when I bump into someone. On instinct, I lift my hand to stop myself from falling over and when my palm lands on a solid muscular chest, a feeling of recognition washes over me.

Looking up, I'm shocked to see who I've just run into.

"Huxley," I breathlessly whisper, and I take the moment to look him over. The bandage on his head is gone and he looks like the Huxley I know and remember, except for the sling on his left arm.

"You're, Kendall." When he says my name, my heart soars until he adds, "right?"

Nodding in agreement, I purse my lips in frustration. I don't know what else to say, he obviously still doesn't remember me, sadly I smile. "How are you?"

"Good," he replies. Wow, one word, that's all I get.

"Taking each day at a time but for the most part, my memory is still..."

He doesn't finish what he was going to say because what else is there to say? He doesn't remember me, yet I remember everything, and seeing him in the flesh makes me realize just how much I miss him and want him.

"How was Hawaii?" he asks, snapping me to the present and away from my pity party for one.

"Good."

"Good," he repeats.

If either one of us says good again, I'm gonna lose my shit. Why is this so awkward?

My flight is called and I'm thankful for the escape. "That's my flight," I tell him. "It was good to see you." Without waiting for his reply, I step around him and speed walk the rest of the way to my gate.

My heart is rapidly racing and it's not from the speed walk. It's from seeing *him*. He's just as hunky as I remember and I hate that he still has no recollection of me, but it cements my decision to move on because this, this is too hard to deal with. But why is there a part of me that feels like I'm making a mistake?

37

KENDALL

...Halloween

"ARE YOU THINKING ABOUT HIM AGAIN?"

"No," I defensively refute but like the billion-and-one times my best friend has asked this in the last, well, since I first met him. And like the previous billion-and-one times before, she knows I'm full of shit...even if we are chatting over the phone right now.

"I call bull poop, Betty Boop." She pauses, and I know what she's going to say next, just from the change in her breathing. "Why don't you just call him?"

"We've had this conversation, repeatedly, and the Huxley part of—"

"Of my life is closed. If I was meant to be in his life, he'd remember me. I've heard it all before, Kendall, and like all the other times, you're full of shit, my lil' chicken-shit." I roll my eyes at that rhyme, but at the same time I grin because that's what Rarns does. She makes me smile when I'm feeling miserable. "Now, do you need me to come over and play fairy godmother and perfect your hair with a do-over?"

"I would love that because right now, my hair looks like I'm an extra on *The Walking Dead*."

"Oh God, please, put down the curling wand and wait for me and my magical hands to arrive and bibbity-bobbity-boo, sexy princess."

"Actually, I decided to go as Red Riding Hood and, Rarns, I'm disappointed no rhyme with bibbity-bobbity-boo."

"You know me, I like to keep you on your toes and a rhyme will pop up when you least expect it to."

"You're lucky I love you."

"Aww, look at you, rhyming on my behalf."

"Just get over here and fix my hair, please?"

"Only 'cause you asked nicely and only because I know you'll have a drink waiting for me...and maybe some Cheetos too."

"You know I always have Cheetos on hand AND since it's Halloween, I also have Sweetarts and taffy."

"Marry me?" she singsongs through the phone.

"You know I love you, Rarns, but I'm all about the D."

"You and me both, girl, you and me both. I'll see you soon, baboon."

Before I can reply and scold her for calling me a baboon, she's hung up. "Bitch," I mumble.

Walking into the kitchen, I start mixing up a pitcher of cosmos for us. I catch a glimpse of my outfit in the hall mirror and my mind drifts to the time Huxley and I were talking about Halloween...

...We're lying naked in bed and I've lost count of the number of orgasms we've had since reuniting earlier today. Yesterday? Two days ago? I actually have no clue as to what time or day it is anymore. My sole focus has been on Huxley and only him.

"What are you dressing up as on Halloween?" he asks out of nowhere.

"Halloween is a few months away yet."

"And if we're going to have amazing costumes, we need to start organizing them now."

"Are we a Halloween fan, Mr. Weston?"

"Proud fan for twenty plus years now."

"You're such a kid."

"Would a kid do what we just did? Repeatedly?"

"Well, noooo." My cheeks darken as I think of all the kinky and sexy things we have done recently.

"My point exactly...and seeing you red just now, I have THE perfect costume for us."

"And what might that be, oh wise Halloween master?"

"You, Red Riding Hood. Me, the Big Bad Wolf."

"You, Tarzan. Me, Jane," I say in a deep gruff voice.

"No! You, Red Riding Hood. Me, the Big Bad Wolf."

"Seriously?"

"Seriously."

"And you know what else?"

"What?"

"When we come back home from partying with our friends, this Big Bad Wolf is going to eat you until you're screaming and then I'll fuck you until you pass out."

"Promises, promises, Mr. Big Bad Wolf."

"Does Lil' Red want a preview of what's to come on

Halloween night?" He waggles his eyebrows at me, and the hunger is his eyes sets my body on fire.

Nodding, I bite my bottom lip. "This Lil' Red definitely wants to see the Big Bad Wolf come out to play."

...Opening my eyes, the memory fades but the feelings are ever present. Then I realize that my hand is up under my skirt and rather than the Big Bad Wolf devouring me, it's my wee red fingers working me over. My fingers are nothing compared to *him* but the memory of *him* and my fingers is enough to send me over the edge, and I climax, murmuring his name like I always do.

Pulling my hand out from under my skirt, I turn around and slide down the kitchen cabinets to the floor. My heart is racing and breaking at the same time. How can an orgasm be laced with sadness? I hate that he doesn't remember me because I really thought he was my Prince Charming. "Fucking fairy tales," I grumble, and then I laugh because I'm attending a Halloween party dressed as Red Riding Hood...from a fucking fairy tale.

Standing up, I walk into my bathroom and wash my hands. Looking at my reflection, my cheeks are flushed. No sooner have I finished rinsing my hands, there's a knock at my door. "Coming," I yell.

Swinging the door open, I'm met with a sexy as hell devil/angel. "Fuck me, Rarns, you look amazing." One half of her is virginal white—angel, and the other, fiery red, devil—and they blend in the middle creating one hell of a costume.

"Says the sexy one." She steps past me and places a kiss on my cheek. "We are definitely finding a wolf to chow down on you tonight."

"I don't need a wolf when I have these," I wriggle my fingers at her, "and a drawer full of fun."

"Who says you can't play with a wolf AND use all of those?"

"Clearly I'm talking to the devil within right now."

"Babe, you and I both know that those virgins are the dirtiest of them all. They are just waiting for their inner sexy devil to appear."

"Whatever you say. Now, let's fix my hair and go get our drink on."

"I like your style, Red. I like your style."

She links her arm with mine. We stop off at the kitchen and grab the pitcher of cosmo and two glasses, and head into my en suite where Rarns works her magic and turns my rat's nest into perfect Red Riding Hood waves.

It's packed in Prohibition tonight and everyone, I mean everyone, is dressed up. Rarns and I make a beeline for the bar and my favourite bartender is working this evening. "Looking good, Red," Embry greets me as I lean on the bar.

"You too, Batman, you too."

"The usual?"

"Please...and keep 'em coming."

"You got it, Red." Nodding, I turn around and lean against the wooden bar.

Looking around, I take in all the costumes and then freeze because I see the sexiest of all sexy wolves standing there. Prohibition is packed but within the crowd, somehow, we've managed to connect. I stand here frozen and stare at the man who still owns my heart. At the man who is dressed as a wolf, just like we discussed when we were still a we.

He licks his bottom lip and the silver ball on the end of his tongue shines in the light and memories of him, his tongue, and that little ball from when we discussed this very night flash within my mind.

Swallowing deeply, I lick my bottom lip and even though he's on the other side of the room, I can feel his eyes watch my tongue dart out and swipe across my lip.

The spell is broken when someone taps my shoulder, looking back I see Embry has placed my drink on the bar. "Thanks," I utter and when I look back to where Huxley was, he's gone. "Did I imagine that?" I mumble to myself as I turn around, lean against the bar, and pick up my drink.

"No, you did not imagine that," Embry informs me. "There's an undeniable connection there and even if he doesn't remember you from before, he wants you now."

"How can you be so sure?" I hesitantly ask.

"Because he's right behind you." As he says those words, I feel him behind me. Closing my eyes, I take a deep breath and soak up his presence. Spinning around, I come face-to-face with Huxley. My wolf. Silently we stare at one another. It's intense. It's all-consuming and I wish for some sort of recognition to flicker in his eyes, but there's nothing.

"Hi," I shyly utter.

"Hi," he replies, and that one word vibrates through my body. Every nerve ending fires as if a shot of rocket fuel has been injected into my veins. There's a magnetic pull between us and I find myself being pulled toward him.

"Westie, where's my drink?" a feminine voice says, and I falter until I see Bryce waddle up beside him. When she sees me, she screeches my name like a banshee and pulls me in for a hug. "Holy duckbills, Kendall, you're the hottest Red I have ever seen."

"And your costume is the freakin' best." She's dressed as a rainbow with a pot of gold, and the pot of gold is her now massive bump. "I just love it." From behind her, Hayden arrives and he's dressed as a leprechaun. "Oh, my god, you two are the cutest." And then I remember if Huxley and I were together, we'd look cute and amazing too.

"How have you been, girl? Feels like forever since I've seen you."

"We had lunch together last week."

"That was forever ago," she whines. Then she looks to Huxley. "Where's my drink, dude?"

"Ummm, I..." he stammers, "I got side-tracked."

Turning my gaze to his, I see that he's still staring at me.

"You're lucky I love your ass, but ne—" She cuts herself off from talking when she notices the two of us staring at one another.

Deciding to take a chance, I step closer to my big bad wolf. I grip his cheeks in my palms and kiss him. I put every bit of me into it. His tongue slides into my mouth and I smile into the kiss.

Kissing him is exactly as I remember and like always when we kiss, everything around me fades away.

Vaguely I hear Bryce, "Holy shit, if I wasn't already pregnant, I would be after that kiss."

"Bryce," Hayden scolds her, "way to ruin the moment."

Huxley pulls away from me.

Both of us breathing heavily.

He stares at me. Blinking rapidly and from the blank look on his face, our kiss didn't spark anything.

Not wanting to hear him tell me he still doesn't remember, I turn on my heel and run away. My heart once again breaking, but this time it's my fault for giving in to temptation.

Fuck temptation.

Fuck fate.

Fuck fairy tales, but most of all, fuck love!

38

HUXLEY

STANDING HERE SHOCKED that she just kissed me, I watch her race away. My heart is racing in a way that I've never felt before. That kiss did nothing for my memory, but it brought my body alive.

Someone smacks me up the side of my head. Looking toward my assailant, I see Bryce staring daggers at me. *What the fuck did I do now?* Her eyebrows raised and her facial expression murderous, uh oh, I'm in trouble. That's confirmed when she snaps, "Go after her, you fool."

I stare at her dumbfounded, but her words spark something inside of me and I do as she suggested. Turning on my heel, I chase after Red. The origins of the fairy tale not lost on me as I exit Prohibition and chase Kendall down the street and around the corner. "Kendall," I call out and the sound of my voice causes her steps to falter, and she stumbles, falling down on the pavement.

Racing over to her, I offer her my hand and help her back to her feet. She lifts her gaze and I see tears streaking down her cheeks. Reaching out, I swipe my thumb across her cheek. "Kendall—"

"You...you called me Kendall," she blubbers.

"That's your name, isn't it?" I scrunch my face in confusion.

"Well yeah, but..."

"But what?"

"But you don't remember me, yet you know my name."

"Ummm." Lifting my hand, I squeeze the back of my neck. "I remember from the hospital and airport," I pause, "Bryce, umm, ahh, told me to come after you."

"Oh." That one word is laced with such sadness it cuts me deep down, but why does the fact she's upset cut me. "So, you still don't—"

Shaking my head side to side, I confirm to her that I still have no clue who she is.

"Oh," she repeats again.

"But I feel something," I honestly tell her, hoping that my honesty softens the blow of having no memory of her. Of us.

"Oh," she utters again and like the other two times, she sounds so broken.

"I'm sorry," I offer. I know sorry won't ease the pain currently radiating from her, but I need her to know that I am. I hate I'm causing her agony and I hate even more so that there's not a fucking thing I can do about it.

"Why are you sorry?"

"Because I don't remember you."

"O—" I can't take hearing that from her again, so I interrupt her, "Yeah, oh." She laughs, and fuck me sideways, it's musical and I find myself grinning for the first time since chasing after her. "You have a beautiful laugh."

"Thanks," she timidly replies. Wiping the last of the tears away.

We both fall silent and stare at one another. Neither of us saying a word. Each of us broken in different ways.

"Huxley," she voices just as I say, "Kendall."

We both laugh and again, the sound is bliss to my ears. "You go first," she quickly says, pulling my focus back to her.

"Do you think, maybe, we can, ummm, get coffee sometime?"

Her eyes widen and then the biggest smile graces her fucking gorgeous face. "I'd love to get coffee with you sometime."

"Okay, good."

"Good."

We silently stare at one another and it's getting awkward. "Should we go back inside?"

"Yeah," she nods, "I'm freezing my titties off out here."

My eyes drop to her chest, and I see her nipples pointing through her top. Lifting my gaze back to hers, I shrug at the expression on her face right now, but hey, I'm a guy and she mentioned tits. "Well, we can't have that happen to such gorgeous titties. It's my civic duty to escort you and your titties back inside."

"I'm surprised you're not offering to warm them up for me."

"Well, I'm happy to oblige if you so wish." My gaze

drops back to her breasts, I notice that her chest is heaving right now. *Is she turned on?*

"My tits and I are fine for now, but I will keep that under advisement." She turns on her heel, and silently we walk back to Prohibition.

"Do I need to kill him?" her friend asks her.

She shakes her head. "No killing necessary. It's all good." Her voice is soft and dare I say, less broken.

"So, you two..." Bryce asks without asking, flicking her finger between us.

"Are friends," I offer, and I see Kendall flinch at my words.

"I need a drink," she states and turns toward the bar. I go to follow her, but Bryce puts her hand on my chest, halting me.

"Let her go."

"But—"

"But nothing, sit your ass down and have a beer." Bryce gives me the 'mom' look and I comply. She squeezes my shoulder. "She needs time to adjust to being friends or whatever the hell you two are."

Nodding, I look over to the bar and focus on her. Her friend is next to her and it looks like she's crying again. Her shoulders are moving up and down and her head hangs down in defeat. I did that to her, and I feel like a shithead. She's upset because of me and my stupid memory, well, lack of memory.

I'm so glad that I'm not going back to the rigs, I need to be here to try and remember her, or at the very least, let myself fall for her again. I feel a connection with this woman, yet I have no fucking recollection of ever knowing her, but my body reacts when she's around like it knows her. Like it wants her. Needs her. But my mind is in a completely different fuzzy universe. From the little I know about Kendall, I want her just as much as I want my memories. But does she still want me?

39

KENDALL

AFTER ORDERING a round of shots and another cosmo, I rest my elbows on the bar and lower my head in defeat. I feel Rarns slide in next to me. "It's so hard, Rarns," I cry as I wait for my drinks. "I want to be around him, hoping to spark some memory of me, but it's just so hard having him not remember anything."

I begin to cry harder.

Our shots are placed in front of us and needing to feel numb, I pick the two up. One in each hand and one after the other, I shoot them back. "Two more, Embry," I ask as he places my cosmo down.

He nods and refills them.

This time, I hand one to Rarns. "Bottoms up." I raise my glass in a salute and chug it back. The tequila once again sears its way down my esophagus, but I cherish the burn because it makes me focus on that and not the sexy as fuck wolf who is currently staring at me across the bar. Even with my back to him, I can feel his gaze on me.

"You okay?" Rarns squeezes my forearm and my eyes well with tears again.

"Yes. No. I don't fucking know."

"Well, if it makes you feel better, there's still a massive-ass spark between the two of you."

"But he doesn't remember!"

"But there's a spark and that's got to count for something, right?"

Looking to my friend, I sigh. "What do I do, Rarns?"

"Babe, I can't tell you what to do. You need to follow your heart."

"But what if it breaks again?"

"But what if it doesn't?"

She picks up my cosmo and walks away, leaving me to ponder her words just now. Ordering another cocktail, I decide that I'll leave it to fate. She seems to have some warped and wicked plan for Huxley and me, maybe we will finally get our chance. I mean, she can't be that much of a bitch, right?

With my cocktail in hand, I walk back over to the group. "Hey," I greet Huxley when he stands up. "Mind if I join you?"

"That's fine," he replies. He shuffles over, allowing me to sit next to him.

"Thanks," I say, taking a seat next to him. "I'm, umm, sorry about before."

"You have nothing to be sorry for. This whole thing is fucked."

"That's one way of putting it."

Silence envelops us while the rest of the table happily chats away. I keep staring at him out of the corner of my eye and each time, I catch him staring back at me.

I laugh, "This is so awkward, Hux. You and I..." I drift off, not sure if I should broach our past or not.

"You and I what?" he pushes me.

"We always chatted and it flowed but this, it's..."

"Awkward."

"Yeah, that." I laugh again. "How do we go from here?"

"Well, we chat and get to know one another."

"Okay, I guess we can try that."

Again, we fall silent, but this time, it's a little less awkward. "How's work?" I ask him. It was the first thing that came to my mind and then I internally berate myself because he can't work anymore.

"Really good, actually. Hayden and I have new jobs. Rather than being in the field and on the tools, we are now based in an office here."

"Doing what?"

"I'm now planning and scheduling upcoming maintenance and Hayden produces the permits for the work I have scheduled."

"So, you're office jocks now."

"Pretty much."

"Don't you miss being in the field? In the thick of it?"

"Yes and no."

"How so?"

"Prior to the incident, I vaguely remember not being happy. Apparently Hayd and I had been talking before the accident and we agreed we were ready for a change. I think that's why the accident happened; I wasn't focused."

"No," Hayden interrupts. "It was a freak accident because someone let go of the line. You are the most focused person I know when we're out there."

"You have to say that—"

"I don't have to say shit. I've read the report and I know you."

"Agree to disagree, anyway, as I was saying. Hayd and I approached Troy about our concerns. He said he knew it was coming and had been speaking with Aurora Energy here in the city. They were looking for new planners and schedulers. Hayden and I met with them, and the rest is history."

"That's amazing, so you're based here in the city now?"

"Yep, occasionally we'll need to head to site, mostly when the maintenance shutdowns occur, but these jobs take a year or more of planning."

"Really, that long?"

"Yep, it's not like you can go to Walmart and get a twenty-inch valve or a turbine off the shelf. These things need to be ordered and engineered."

"Wow, that's, I had no clue."

"Are you talking shop, Huxley Weston?" Bryce scolds me.

"No, I'm chatting with Kendall...about our jobs and shit."

"Fine, I'll allow it, but can we maybe talk about something else?"

"Like what? Baby shit?" Hux teases.

"No," she snaps at him. "Maybe about how my Gems just beat your Crushers."

"You're a Crushers fan?" I ask him.

Nodding, he smiles. "Yep, sure am. Proud fan since ninety-two."

"Me too. They're smashing it this season, well except for last night's game." Then I look to Bryce. "And you just lost awesomeness points for your team choice, well, lack thereof choice."

"At least my team is Canadian."

"What's that got to do with it?"

"Support local," she sasses back at me.

"Local would be supporting the Vikings since we live in Vancouver." I shudder as that team's name passes my lips and when I look around, everyone's face is turned up at that. The Vikings might be our city's team but to put it nicely, they suck. "So glad Kallen signed with the Crushers and not the Vikings."

"At least we all agree the Viking's suck," Bryce says, and everyone nods their head in agreement. Then Bryce's eyes widen, and she snaps her head toward me. "Isn't Kallen's last name Jones?"

I nod and wait for her to make the connection. "Are you related to him?"

Nodding, I smile. "He's my baby brother."

"You mean, Kallen Jones, NY Crushers goalie, was with us on Canada Day?"

"Yep," I reply, letting the 'p' pop and a smile graces my face at the love they all have for my brother.

"But...but...how did I not place him?" she asks, confusion marring her face.

"'Cause the dick lost a bet to JJ and had to shave his head and grow that creepy ass mo. He looked like a freakin serial killer."

"True, he looked terrible with a bald head. He needs his luscious chocolate locks to finish him off." She gets a dreamy look on her face.

"I'll have to take your word on that." I look to Huxley. "I'm more of a dirty blond kind of gal."

He smiles at my comment but makes no move...and I don't know how I feel about that.

The rest of the evening passes by in a blur, a drunken fantabulous blur, but I can say it was the most fun I've had in a very long time. Huxley and I flirt with one another but neither of us makes any sexual moves...even though I want to throw myself at him and ride him like the stallion he is. Looks like BOB will be getting a workout when I get home later.

We all say our goodbyes and since I live only a few blocks away, Huxley offers to walk me home. We walk in silence for the first few blocks, but as my building comes into view, he tugs on my hand and stops me. "I had a really nice time tonight, Kendall."

"I had a nice time too, Hux."

"You know, I hate when people call me Hux but when you do, I don't mind it at all."

"You've told me that before," I whisper.

We stare at one another and like a moth to a flame, we drift closer together.

"I really want to kiss you," he says, breaking the silence.

"And I really want you to kiss me, Hux."

He cups my cheek, lowers his head down, and kisses me. My eyes close and everything around me fades into the background. It's just Huxley and me. It's perfect. Everything is perfect. Until he breaks our kiss and stares back at me, blankly. With one vacant look, my heart crushes...again.

"Good night," I quickly say and then I race down the street to my building. Letting myself in, I step into the elevator. Pressing the button for my floor, I lean my head against the wall and let the first tear drop.

Why do I keep doing this to myself? I need to stop getting my hopes up that he'll remember. Maybe, it's time that I forget him. We may have a connection physically but without his memories, I mean nothing to him. Huxley and me as a couple are officially over.

40

KENDALL

...New Year's Eve

IT'S New Year's and like last year, Rarns and I are back at Prohibition, with plans to meet up with Bryce. The crazy lady is ready to give birth any day now and she still wants to party it up on New Year's Eve with the rest of us. "One last hurrah" were her exact words when we met for coffee just before Christmas.

After my magnificent kiss last New Year's, I thought I'd be all loved up tonight but fate—bitch—had other plans and once again, I'm single...and ready to mingle...so I'm telling (lying to) Rani. How sad am I?

After the disaster that was Halloween, I stood to my word, and I've stayed away from Huxley. Well, as much as I could when my new friend's husband just so happens to be his best friend.

Bryce and I have become good friends. It was hard to see her and not see *him*. However, Bryce was a champ, and we'd meet up at a coffee shop near her business or somewhere where *he* wouldn't be, BUT that didn't always work out. Let me tell you, it was hard each and every time. Each time my eyes would land on him, I'd hold out hope that he'd remember, hell, I'd even be happy for him to fall in love with me again. And it always screwed me up for a few days after because I didn't know how to act around him; it's no wonder he didn't fall in love with me again.

As time went on, I thought I was okay with us not being an us anymore, but then I'd see him again and I'd be right back to square one. Pining over a guy who doesn't remember me was hard, and unlike in the movies, he hasn't fallen hopelessly back in love with me.

There's no rule book when it comes to the guy you love not remembering you or loving you back, so I was navigating this alone. *Screw you, Google.*

Bryce informed me that Huxley's memory is coming back in jumbled pieces. He's starting to remember things here and there, but there's no rhyme or reason to what returns. He now remembers Bryce and how she and Hayden got together. So I hold out hope that one of these days he'll remember me too, but we hardly knew one another before his accident, so those memories I think will be lost forever.

What's weird is that I'm pretty sure he feels something for me but he's holding back, and I don't know why. Maybe, I'll just kiss him seven times like he demanded last year when the clock strikes twelve and BOOM, he'll remember, but I'm not living in a fairy tale and magic like that never happens in real life.

As soon as Rani and I walk into Prohibition, my eyes

immediately home in on *him,* and fuck me sideways, he looks hot as fuck tonight. Then again, he always looks hot as fuck.

Like last year, we grab our free drink, chug the shitty warm liquid back, and make a beeline for the bar to remove the shitty taste it leaves in our mouths. "Why do we always drink this free shit upon arrival?" I ask Rarns as we make our way to the bar.

"'Cause it's free," she nonchalantly says as we squeeze between a couple already making out. "Save it for midnight, peoples," Rarns throws at them as we walk on by.

My gaze once again lands on *him* and I start to regret coming tonight. I should have stayed home with a bottle of Sour Puss and a bag of Cheetos. I don't want to be thinking of *him* and the amazingness we had last year. I need liquid courage to get through tonight. However, I know one thing, I'm still unequivocally in love with him and having the person you love not love you back, or even remember you, is hard to swallow.

"Shots," I shout as we reach the bar.

Rarns slaps the bar and grins at me. "I knew you were my bestie for a reason." She turns her attention to the barmaid. "Four shots of tequila and a cosmo." She looks to me. "And what do you want, Kendall?"

"The same," I say with a shrug, not really sure what I want to drink. All I know is that I need a drink to wash away that shitty champagne taste.

"So, that's eight shots and two cosmos," she tells her. I shake my head at my bestie's enthusiasm.

The barmaid places our shots down first and then she

starts to make our cocktails. Rani hands me one. "Goodbye shitty year, hello fun year." We clink our glasses together and do our shots.

I shudder. Then I pick up another one and shoot it back too, may as well keep the burn going. Shaking my head, I blink a few times and on the other side of the bar, I see Huxley.

He's staring at me intently. I smile and he smiles back, but it's his generic one. Not the one that lights up his face or sets my insides quivering. Call me stupid, but I was hoping that if our gaze met while here, like last year, the same thing would occur but nope, nothing.

Turning my attention back to the bar, I sink my remaining two shots, deciding that I'm going to get absolutely shitfaced tonight and bring in the new year drunk as a skunk. I don't need a man to bring in the new year with, I'm a strong and independent woman who has a BOB, I'll be fine.

41

HUXLEY

PROHIBITION IS PACKED TONIGHT. We were lucky to grab the booth we have but Bryce can be persuasive and a pregnant, ready-to-pop Bryce, fuck me, she's deadly.

Hayden and I are on our way back from the bar with the first round of drinks and shots when I see Kendall. She looks absolutely beautiful tonight, but then again, she does every time I see her. However, there's a sadness in her eyes and that's due to me and my missing memories. I'd like to get to know her better, but I can only imagine that it would be hard for her. I'd be experiencing all these firsts but for her, they wouldn't be firsts.

We reach the booth and I place the drinks tray down when someone bumps into me. I lose my balance, and in slow motion, stumble and fall. I see the table coming toward me and before I can stop the collision, I hit my head on the corner of the booth and with a thud, I land face down on the floor.

Darkness envelops me, but it's different to the last

time, this time in amongst the misty shadows, images flash before me like an old-school home video. My first time seeing a blowout. The explosion with Hayden. His and Bryce's wedding. Boarding up Grouse Mountain. Seeing Kendall for the first time. Kissing Kendall. Fucking Kendall. Canada Day with Kendall. I see it all. I see everything involving Kendall.

Groaning, I roll over to my back and stare up at the ceiling. Blinking rapidly as everything comes back into focus and my memories continue to reload in my brain.

A smile graces my face because I remember. "I remember," I whisper, covering my head with my arm.

"Shit, Westie, you okay?" Hayden says from above, his voice laced with concern. Moving my arm, I see him staring down at me, he looks worried. He offers me his hand and pulls me up into a standing position.

"I remember," I repeat again.

Bryce's eyes widen but I don't have a chance to discuss it because the hairs on the back of my neck prickle. "She's nearby," I mumble.

Spinning around, everything becomes fuzzy when I spin too quickly, but I glance across the bar and my eyes immediately find her, my Kissy Kendall. I stare at her, mesmerized by her beauty.

A force overtakes my body and as if I'm Moses, like the Red Sea people step out of the way, parting to allow me to reach my girl.

She looks up and smiles and just like this time last year, everything around me fades away and it's only her that I see. Stopping before her, I smile. Flashing her my pearly whites because I cannot remember the last time, I felt like this. Yes, I can, it was the last time I was with Kendall before I left. "You look beautiful tonight, Kissy Kendall."

"Thanks, yo—" Her eyes widen when she realizes what I just called her. She stumbles backward in shock, reaching out, I grab onto her arm and steady her. A jolt of electricity zaps through me when I touch her. "Wwwwww...what did you call me?"

Lifting my hand from her arm, I cup her face, running the pad of my thumb over the apple of her cheek. "I called you, Kissy Kendall."

"You remember?" she whispers, tears welling in her eyes.

Nodding, I stare at the woman that I irrefutably love. "I remember everything, Kendall, and...and I need to tell you something."

"What?"

"I love you, Kissy Kendall. I love you with all my heart, soul, and everything in between."

A stray tear falls down her cheek, I wipe it away.

"I love you too, Hunky Huxley."

"Still not a fan of that name but you love me, and I remember. That's all I care about."

"You really remember?" she questions again, still in shock and not quite believing me.

"I remember every sexy X-rated detail, Kissy Kendall Jones. Now, should we do a practice kiss for midnight?"

She shakes her head. "No, this is no practice kiss. This is the kiss of our forever."

She grips my face between her hands and presses her lips to mine. Wrapping my arms around her waist, I pull her to me and deepen the kiss and our connection. My tongue sweeps into her mouth and I feel like I've come home. I'm right where I'm meant to be.

"Hi," she breathlessly murmurs when we pull apart.

"Hi."

"You really, really remember?"

"I really, really do."

We stare at one another; I've never felt joy like I do right in this moment. "I'm never letting you go, Kendall Jones. I was hooked after one kiss—"

"One kiss just wasn't enough," she says with a grin.

"Neither was seven, if I remember."

"Our first seven kisses were pretty good but, Huxley Weston, I will never tire of kissing you. Now kiss me again."

"Yes, ma'am."

Covering her mouth with mine, I kiss her like my life depends on it. This woman is it for me...but I'm not Hayden, I'm not going to marry her right now but one day I will. One day she will be mine forever, but for now, I'm going to kiss her like she's never been kissed before.

42

KENDALL

HE REMEMBERS.

He remembers me.

He's kissing me.

He's kissing me just like he used to.

Holy shit, he remembers.

This is the best night ever. Coming up for air, I stare into his gorgeous hazel eyes. "Is this really real?" I ask him. "You remember?"

"It's really real, I remember. Everything."

Lifting my hand, I pinch his arm and his eyes widen. "Ouch, what the hell, Kendall?"

"Just making sure I wasn't dreaming."

"If I remember correctly, I did that to you on St. Patrick's Day and Bryce hit me for pinching you."

"Actually, Hayden did and then he—"

"Said something about poking." He waggles his eyebrows at me, and I'm tempted to take him into the back room and let him poke me. A megawatt smile is stuck on my face right now because he remembers. Tears of happiness pour down my cheeks because he just told me a story of us. "You really remember," I tearfully repeat.

"Really, really."

"Aww, they Shrek'd each other again," Bryce says from beside me; I hadn't even noticed that she'd joined us. Actually, all of our friends have joined us. "I'm so freakin' happy I could burst." The timing of that statement could not have been more perfect because suddenly liquid gushes all around us.

"Did you literally just burst?" Huxley asks her.

"Ummm, no. I think my water just broke." She looks to Hayden, wide-eyed and in shock.

"Now?" he asks her.

"Yep, now."

We all stand here in shock. My eyes flick between Hayden and Bryce, waiting for one of them to move, but it seems they're both frozen. "Sooo," I voice but Bryce interrupts me.

"Dude, I cannot have this baby in a bar, you need to get me to the hospital noooooooow." She screeches that last word like a banshee and bends over, holding her stomach as the first contraction hits.

Everyone remains silent.

All eyes are on Bryce.

She stands back up straight, well as straight as you can when you're in labor. "Move your flippin' ass, Hayden Bowden," she growls through clenched teeth. "No bar born baby for us."

At that statement, Hayden jumps into action and escorts his wife out of Prohibition, and we all follow like lost little sheep. Hayden and Bryce jump into the taxi that just so happened to be waiting out front, and the rest of us wait for the Uber that Danny has just ordered.

Huxley wraps his arms around me from behind and I snuggle into him.

Finally, I feel at peace.

Everything is right in the world once again.

Bryce and Hayden are about to welcome their baby boy—I'm convinced it's a boy.

But most of all, Huxley remembers.

Everyone is chatting around us, but my eyes are closed and I'm focusing on the man holding me in his arms right now. I'd love nothing more than to take him back to my apartment and bring in the new year, just the two of us, but Bryce is about to have her baby and we need to be there for our friends. I'm sure he and I can sneak off to a supply closet and celebrate us being us again and him remembering. I mean, it's not like we haven't gotten it on before in public.

Our Uber arrives and we all climb into the car. Huxley is sitting next to me and he pulls me into his side, there's not an inch of breath between us. Ever since his memories have returned, he hasn't let go of me. And I'm not complaining one bit.

We arrive at the hospital, and thirty minutes later, Mackenna Bowden comes screaming into the world. Once Bryce is settled, we all congregate in her room. Us girls are cooing over sweet little Mackenna, who is NOT a boy like I thought, and the guys congratulate Hayden for holding Bryce's hand while she pushed a watermelon out of her hoo-ha.

Everyone is still congratulating them when Rarns notices the time on the clock.

"Ten!" she shouts, and then we all continue with the countdown.

Nine

Eight

Seven

Six

Five

Four

Three

Two

One

"Happy New Year," everyone sings out, causing Mackenna to startle and wail like her mom did earlier this evening when her first contraction hit.

"Happy New Year, Kissy Kendall Jones."

"Happy New Year, Hunky Huxley."

Huxley grips my cheeks and slams his lips against mine in an all-encompassing kiss that leaves me breathless and light-headed. "That reminds me of our New Year's kiss last year."

He rests his forehead against mine and murmurs, "That's New Year's kiss number one...only six to go."

"You and your seven kisses," I playfully tease.

"One just wasn't enough, now pucker up, babe."

I press my lips to his again, not caring that our friends

are currently catcalling and telling us to get a room. Huxley flips them the bird and continues to kiss me.

This isn't how I planned my New Year's turning out, but I wouldn't change it for the world because Mackenna Bowden was born, Huxley remembers me, and I got a New Year's kiss, well seven, that I'll never forget.

EPILOGUE

...Seven years later
...New Year's Eve

"HURRY UP, we're gonna be late," I yell out to Huxley and the girls.

"Coming," Ainsley and Ciara singsong in unison. For non-fraternal twins, they sure are so much alike, in both looks and temperament.

"I'm going to head over to reception so they don't leave without us. Hux, please don't dawdle...or let those two lead you astray."

"Yes, dear," he shouts, and then I'm met with giggles, so I just know that we're going to be late.

Pulling on my coat, I race through the resort to reception. It's really chilly tonight, and I begin to wonder if maybe it will be too cold for the girls. They are only little after all.

Heading to the coffee shop, I order two coffees and

two hot chocolates. At least we can have warm drinks while on the tour to bring in the new year.

For something different, and now that the girls are older, we travelled abroad to Lapland and are once again staying at Apukka Resort. Rather than in an aurora cabin, we are in their family suite. The last time Huxley and I were here, under the northern lights, he proposed...while we were naked...after sharing seven kisses on New Year's, which has become a tradition of ours.

I fall more and more in love with this man each and every day. We came so close to losing our happily ever after and it just makes me hold on to him that much tighter.

We're letting the girls stay up tonight because well, it's New Year's and we're in Lapland, so why not? Plus, we've booked an Across the Arctic Night by Reindeer tour, and Huxley being Huxley, managed to sweet talk them into allowing us to be in the middle of the Arctic for the cross over into the new year.

I'm waiting for our drinks when the hairs on the back of my neck prickle and stand on end. A feeling of déjà vu washes over me and when I turn around my eyes land on my Hottie McHotterson husband. Huxley and the girls are racing toward me. My mind drifts to the airport in Hawaii when I first felt like this, and my eyes spied Hottie McHotterson, and then it morphs to the coffee shop at the Seattle airport.

My mouth drops open in shock. "It was you," I whisper to myself.

"Who was me?" Huxley asks as he and the girls stop next to me.

"At the airport." He looks at me, confused. "Twice at airports I saw a Hottie McHotterson and we had a moment and the hairs on my neck prickled."

"And it was me?"

"I'm positive it was you because, just now, that same feeling washed over me, and rather than it be a fleeting thing, you're here."

"And so are we," Ainsley adds.

"Yes you are baby girl." I look back at Huxley. "It was you, both times. I'm sure of it."

"So fate was messing with us and we didn't even know it."

"Fate's such a bitch," I add, garnering a sound of shock from Ciara.

"Mommy said a bad word."

"Mommy did and I'm sorry, but it's true. Fate tried to mess with Mommy and Daddy, but we proved to her otherwise."

"Yeah, we did." Huxley wraps his arms around me and stares into my eyes. That prickling feeling intensifies and now I'm more than convinced that it was him. "We proved to fate that we were meant to be and we got our happily ever after."

"Just like Prince Charming and the princess," Ciara says, beaming.

"Just like in the fairy tale," I confirm.

Huxley grips my cheeks and kisses me. It's definitely not a PG kiss, but I don't care. I love kissing him and I will never tire of kissing him.

He pulls back and stares at me. "I love you, Kissy Kendall."

"I love you too, Hunky Huxley. Now kiss me again because..."

"One kiss just isn't enough," we both repeat.

He kisses me again and the moment is broken when our guide tells us it's time to go.

Two hours later, we're in the middle of nowhere. It's pitch-black around us but the sky is lit up, the northern lights are putting on an amazing show tonight.

"It's nearly time," the guide tells us, and he brings the sleigh to a stop. He climbs out and begins to set up a picnic under the stars.

"This wasn't in the brochure." I look inquisitively at my husband, but he just shrugs. He climbs out of the sleigh first and helps the girls down. He tells me to wait and from the tone in his voice, he has something up his sleeve. He turns and escorts them over to the picnic blanket.

Once the girls are settled, he saunters over to me, and I take the opportunity to check out my sexy husband. You'd think being an office jock he would have let himself go but nope, not my husband. I think he's in better shape than ever before.

"M'lady?" he says in a really bad accent when he reaches me in the sleigh. It's such a bad accent that I have no clue what accent he was trying to do.

Standing up, I curtsey and take his outstretched

hand. I step onto the side rail, and he wraps his arms around me.

"Ten," the guide shouts.

And then the girls eagerly start to count backward, excitedly jumping up and down.

Nine

Eight

Seven

Six

Five

Four

Three

Two

One

"Happy New Year," we all sing out into the night sky.

I stare down at my husband, who is still holding me in his arms. "Happy New Year, Hunky Huxley."

"Happy New Year, Kissy Kendall Weston nee Jones, now, gimme my seven kisses."

"So demanding," I tease, but I lower my head down and kiss him. "One," I murmur against his lips.

Once we've gotten in our seven kisses, we make our way over to our girls and sit with them on the picnic blanket and soak it all in.

I'm living my happily ever after with the man of my dreams, our twin girls...and another on the way—and I'm positive it's a boy. Surely, I won't be wrong for a third time.

I admit that I was incorrect about fairy tales because I'm living proof that they do indeed come true and do happen in real life. They really aren't just confined to books and movies.

THE END!

Read on for a sneak peek at Seven Nights, Bryce and Hayden's whirlwind romance.

CHAPTER ONE

HAYDEN

BOOM!

The explosion rips through the rig: scaffolding, tools, and shit flying everywhere. The blast is massive and ripples can be felt for kilometers. The heat from the blast is intense. Every man and woman on the rig is on high alert, scrambling to safety. This is a rig worker's worst fear, a blowout.

Lying on my back, the wind has been knocked out of me. I stare at nothing. I breathe deeply and all I smell is smoke. As I lie amongst the debris, I thank my lucky stars I'm on a rig in Alberta and not in the North Sea. I don't fancy evacuating into a lifeboat—actually, I don't fancy evacuating at all—but at least I'm over dry land.

Nearby, I hear my best friend and bunkmate, Huxley, groan. My eyes land on him, just as his eyes snap open. Another explosion detonates nearby, shock waves rippling around us. He rolls to his side, his eyes darting around the scene before him. "Hayden!" he shouts, as another explosion erupts around us. "Hayden!" he yells again. I want to reply but nothing is coming out of my mouth. My ears are ringing. Black and white spots dot my vision. My breathing is rapid. He bellows my name over and over. Eventually, I manage to catch his attention when I move, the action causing pain to radiate throughout my body. When the first explosion happened, my body was thrown into the scaffolding, a toolbox landing on top of me as I fell to the grid mesh flooring.

"Fuck, Hayden," he hollers, as he climbs over debris to where I'm trapped. Again, I try to speak but nothing comes out. Our eyes lock and his face drains of all colour. I knew it was bad but seeing his face like that confirms my worst fear: I'm trapped on a rig that is literally falling apart around me. I'm helpless to do anything.

"Hayden, man, I'm here, you just hang on, dude." Running his hand over his face he adds, "You better not die on me, fucker."

A sound erupts from me, I think it was a laugh, but with the ringing in my ears, to me it sounds more like a groaning cough. "I'll take that as a yes," Huxley replies, as he throws rubble to the side trying to free me. All of a sudden, I feel free and light, but at the same time there is a heavy weight crushing me when I hear him mumble, "Fuuuuck."

"Huxley? Hayden? That you?" I hear George, the shift supervisor, from behind me yell. Again, I go to reply but nothing comes out. I groan in frustration. George and Huxley do the manly hug before Huxley inspects

George's head. His head is bleeding and he's covered in blood. He swats away Huxley and says, "Don't worry about me, and let's get Hayden out." I hear Huxley reply but it's distorted and fuzzy. My body becomes cold and I shiver. My eyes heavy, as if a lead weight is pulling them down and then I black out.

Opening my eyes again, I see Huxley above me. He shouts, his voice laced with a mixture of fear and relief, "He's still breathing!"

I groan something that doesn't resemble English, but I inwardly sigh when I realise I can faintly hear Huxley and George talking in the background, in amongst a horrible ringing sound.

"What'd he say?" George asks.

"Fucked if I know, but we need to get this toolbox off him and get the fuck out of here before this place goes up."

They both jump into action and I hear someone say, "On three. One. Two. Three." Together they try to move the metal box that is currently crushing me, but every time it moves, I scream in agony.

"Cookies!" I groan out loud, this time it's clear as a bell that I'm talking about cookies.

"What the fuck? Hayden, it's Huxley. We're gonna get you out of here, buddy. Just stay with me."

Opening my eyes again, I smile. In amongst the chaos, a woman—no an angel—appears before me and I smile. Reaching up, I try to touch her but she's just out of my grasp. Reaching out, I whisper something unrecognisable again.

"We need to get him out and fast. He's delusional at

the moment. He's seeing something, he's smiling like a loon."

My face breaks out into a smile as I close my eyes and see her before me again. My body feels like it's floating. "Hayden. Buddy, can you hear me?"

My eyes flutter open and I see Huxley hovering above me, his face calms when he sees me staring up at him, but they flutter shut once again as I let the darkness take me. When I open my eyes again, the floating sensation has been replaced with jostling, and that's when I realise, I'm being carried. The voices around me are fuzzy, my vision blurry. The ringing has stopped, but now I hear nothing but white noise. Another blast rips through the rig and all of a sudden, I'm flying through the air and then free falling. Landing with a thud on the mesh below, I groan in pain as debris and scaffolding begin to rain down on top of us.

Glancing around, I see George and Huxley lying on the ground. *I'll never forgive myself if anything happens to them,* I think to myself as another blast explodes nearby, the heat this time hotter than hell and a sinking feeling appears in my gut.

Huxley moans and I look toward my best friend and yell, "Go, save yourself. Tell her I love her."

"Who?" he questioningly asks.

BOOM!

I don't get to finish my sentence as a final explosion detonates and everything comes crashing down around us.

A glow appears above me and the biggest smile I have ever seen is beaming down at me, a hand is reaching toward me; that's the last thing I see before darkness engulfs me.

The sun is shining into my room and it feels amazing on my face. Lifting my arms, I stretch and moan as I wake up. When my eyes open, I see I'm in my bedroom, and find myself grinning like a goofball. Last night was the best sleep that I've had in ages–after being in hospital for twelve days—it was so good to finally sleep in my own bed. That's what I missed the most; my bed and my thousand thread count sheets...and decent coffee. But most of all, I missed beer. Huxley tried to sneak me in one, but the Nazi nurse caught him and we both got a stern talking to about mixing alcohol with my meds. As much as I love beer, it wasn't worth the risk...or another lecture. For twelve, long gruelling days, I drank crappy hospital coffee, slept in a shitty hospital bed, with scratchy sheets, and put up with a cranky crabby Nazi nurse.

Rolling over, I look toward the windows and smile again. The view is stunning, and when I realise how close I came to losing my life twelve days earlier, you start to appreciate things in a different way and re-evaluate everything. What I do for a living is a risky job, but I wouldn't have it any other way. I'm a FIFO worker—Fly in/Fly out—and currently I work for McMurray Drilling on their Bass Hill rig, based out of Fort McMurray. Well, I guess I no longer work on that rig after the blowout, *I wonder where I'll be sent when I return to work?* I work a seven on and seven off roster, and I'm so glad to no longer be doing twenty-eight and twenty-eight. Twenty-eight days straight at work is tough going. But Vancouver will always be my home.

Recently, I bought a loft apartment in the Gastown area of Vancouver. As soon as I saw this place, I had to have it. It's the perfect location. I've only just moved in, and I really don't want to go back to work in a week. Physically, I've recovered from my injuries, but mentally is another story. It's time to pull on my big boy briefs and climb back on the proverbial horse, as they say. But for tonight, I'll climb on the wingman wagon and have a night out on the town with my best mate, Huxley "Westie" Weston. Tonight, he and I are going to hit up *Prohibition*. He found it the other night when he was out with friends; it's located within the Rosewood Hotel in downtown Vancouver. Apparently, I have to go to because it's 'fucking amazing.' As long as there is beer and hot chicks, I'll be happy.

After showering, I throw on my jeans, boots, and a black button-down shirt. Run a bit of goofy stuff through my hair, spritz on some *Joop*, grab my wallet and keys, and head downstairs to wait for Huxley to arrive. We are cabbing it tonight, responsible drinking and all that shit. For the first time ever, when I get downstairs he's there and waiting for me. "Dude, are you sick? You're on time," I say, as I climb in beside him.

He flips me the bird and I can't help but laugh. "Fuck off, asshole."

"Dude, you will totally be late to your own funeral."

He looks toward me and purses his lips. "Yeah, I totally will, eh?" He laughs, before adding, "Ready for a night to remember? One that will go down in history as 'the best night ever'?"

With a smile, I nod my head in agreement, and for the first time since Huxley suggested this, I'm looking forward to 'the best night ever.' Boy was he right...tonight changed my life in a way I never expected.

Seven Nights is available to buy now, or read with your Kindle Unlimited subscription.

Want to see Rani get her HEA?
Coming in 2022 is Seven Years.

It was only meant to be a weekend of fun for Rani and Cooper, but one weekend wasn't enough so they agreed to a few more.

One year was all it took for them to fall hopelessly in love. It seemed simple enough, but one accident shattered everything.

They hoped to have forever, but they were about to find out the path to true love is full of surprises.

COMING IN 2022

Nothing beats a kiss on New Years'...how about fifteen?
Fifteen authors bring you fifteen different stories about
chance meetings, the perfect New Year's kiss, and ever-
lasting love in the Chasing Serendipity serial anthology.

By Happenstance by LC Taylor & Allie Rose
Seven Kisses by DL Gallie
Chance Encounter by Tara Lee
One Night Only by Rebecca Barber
All Clues Lead to Forever by Rhiannon Marina
Love Resolute by S.E. Roberts by S.E. Roberts
Kismet by K.L. Ramsey
When the Ball Drops by EmKay Connor
Once Upon a New Year by Angie Cottingham
Sparks and Kisses by Jeanene Robinson
Wild Thing by Lux Miller
Champagne Resolutions by Taya Rune

Kiss & Tale by Imani Jay
When Love Lasts by F. East
Dream House by Katherine Moore

Pucker up, it's going to be a scorching kiss when those fireworks explode.

ACKNOWLEDGMENTS

To my fellow **Chasing Serendipity authors**, thank you for allowing me on the adventure with you all. A special shout out to **LC Taylor** for putting this together.

Tash Drake from **Outlined with Love Designs;** thank you again for a stunning cover and fantastic teasers. You are bloody awesome at what you do and I'm so glad to have found you. Here's to many more projects together.

Karen Hrdlicka from **Barren Acres Editing**; thank you for everything that you do for me.

Lisa Edwards thank you for checking all my I's are dotted and my T's are crossed.

My beta babes **Tara, Sarah, Stef, Lana** and **Vi** I would be lost without you ladies. You give me advice when I second guess everything and you helped to bring this story to life. Thank you from the bottom of my heart.

Troy, my husband, my everything. You really are awesome at what you do and you are an even better husband. Love you long-time dude...and feel free to get a job back in Canada cause I really want to live in Vancouver after researching this book. And thank you for all your FIFO knowledge and making sure I got all the technical stuff right.

To my munchkins, **Piper** and **Kade**. You two are my greatest achievement and I'm so lucky to have you both in my life. Love you long-time guys and I look forward to the day when you are forty and can finally read my books.

And finally, **you, my reader**. This is book number eight, wow. Thank you for taking the chance on lil old me. It's still humbling to see my babies live, but it's even more special when someone reaches out to say that read and enjoyed my world. It's because of you guys that I keep doing this...and the voices in my head won't quit talking but your support is a major reason why I keep writing. So thank you, thank you for reading. I hope you loved Bryce and Hayden as much as I do.

PLAYLIST

Him & I - G-Easzy, Halsey
Last Kiss - Pearl Jam
You Found Me - The Fray
Dance Monkey - Tones and I
Someday - Nickelback
Best Day of my Life - American Authors
Shallow - Lady Gaga, Bradley Cooper
All About That Bass - Meghan Trainor
Chandelier - Sia
We Found Love - Rhiannon, Calvin Harris
Kiss From a Rose - Seal
The Boys of Summer - The Ataris
Sleep Like a Baby Tonight - U2
Something Just Like This - The Chainsmokers, Coldplay
#1 Crush - Garbage
I'm Kissing You - Des'ree
Made to Love You - Dan Owen
Chelsea Dagger - The Fratellis
Kiss the Rain - Billie Myers

Call Me Maybe - Carly Rae Jepsen
Other Side of the World - KT Tunstall
Ironic - Alanis Morissette
F**ckin' Perfect - P!nk
I'll Be There for You - The Rembrandts
A Good Heart - Feargal Sharkey
Whiskey in the Jar - Metallica
Black Horse and the Cherry Tree - KT Tunstall
Just Say Yes - Snow Patrol
Superman (It's Not Easy) - Five For Fighting
Danny Boy (Live) - John Butler Trio
Kiss the Girl - Brent Morgan

This playlist can be found on Spotify.

ALSO BY DL GALLIE

STAND ALONES

Out of Nowhere

Antecedent

Doc Steel

Oops

Off the Books

Fractured: A driven world novel

Deck...the Balls

I Pucking Hate That I Love You - coming 31 January 2022

Seven Nights

Seven Kisses

In the Dark of Night anthology**

Secrets anthology**

**only available in paperback direct from me

FALLING NOVELS

Falling for Dr. Kelly

Falling for Dr. Knight

Falling for Agent Cox

Falling for Agent Cruz

Falling: The Complete Collection

THE UNEXPECTED SERIES

When it comes to love, expect the unexpected

The Unexpected Gift

The Unexpected Letter

The Unexpected Package

The Unexpected Connection

The Unexpected series: The Complete Collection

THE CASTAWAY GROVE COLLECTION

Love has arrived in the Grove

Oasis

Unequivocal Love

Five Words

Broken Rules

...and a few more to come.

The Castaway Grove Collection, Vol 1

THE LIQUOR CABINET SERIES

Liquor has never been so disturbingly saucy

Malt Me (Book 1)

Tequila Healing (Book 2)

Wine Not (Book 3)

The Final Shot (Book 4)

The Liquor Cabinet: Series boxset

FACEBOOK ∼ INSTAGRAM ∼ BOOKBUB

GOODREADS ∼ WEBSITE

dlgallieauthor@outlook.com

Sign up to my newsletter

ABOUT THE AUTHOR

DL Gallie is from Queensland, Australia, but she's lived in many different places all over the world, including the UK and Canada. She currently resides in Central Queensland with her husband and two munchkins. She and  her husband have been together since she was sixteen, and although they drive each other crazy at times, she couldn't imagine her life without him.

Shortly after her son was born, DL began reading again. With encouragement from her husband, she picked up the pen and started writing, and now the voices in her head won't shut up.

DL enjoys listening to music, drinking white wine in the summer, red wine in the winter, and beer all year round. She's also never been known to turn down a cocktail, especially a margarita.

www.ingramcontent.com/pod-product-compliance
Lightning Source LLC
Chambersburg PA
CBHW030617120726
47904CB00006B/1930